A Horse for Kate

Horses and Friends Series

MIRALEE FERRELL

A Horse for Kate

David C Cook

transforming lives together

A HORSE FOR KATE
Published by David C Cook
4050 Lee Vance View
Colorado Springs, CO 80918 U.S.A.

David C Cook Distribution Canada
55 Woodslee Avenue, Paris, Ontario, Canada N3L 3E5

David C Cook U.K., Kingsway Communications
Eastbourne, East Sussex BN23 6NT, England

The graphic circle C logo is a registered trademark of David C Cook.

All Scripture quotations are taken from the King
James Version of the Bible. Public domain.

LCCN 2014948630
ISBN 978-0-7814-1114-1
eISBN 978-1-4347-0896-0

Published in association with Tamela Hancock Murray of the Steve
Laube Agency, 5025 N. Central Ave., #635, Phoenix, AZ 85012

The Team: Don Pape, Ingrid Beck, Ramona Cramer Tucker, Nick
Lee, Amy Konyndyk, Helen Macdonald, Karen Athen
Cover Design: Kirk DouPonce, DogEared Design
Cover Models: Emma Myers, Olivia Frisinger

Printed in the United States of America
First Edition 2015

2 3 4 5 6 7 8 9 10 11

091415

To Kate, my darling granddaughter.
I hope by the time you're old enough
to read these books,
you'll love horses and reading as much as I do.

Chapter One

This was the absolute worst day of Kate Ferris's life. Ever. She hunkered deeper into the backseat of her family's Subaru Outback and glared out the window at the passing scenery. Why did God allow her dad to lose his job in Spokane? And even more important, why hadn't He answered her prayer about staying in the only home she'd known all her life? She dreaded trying to make new friends in this strange place. Staying at her old home with her dog and her family was so much easier.

Her six-year-old brother sat up and thumped on the window. "Horses, Kate. Look." The words were flat and expressionless, but Peter emphasized each one with another tap on the window.

Kate removed her earbuds and peered where he pointed. "Cool." A pasture extended from the two-lane road and off toward the looming, snowcapped Mount Hood. "How many do you see?"

"Eleven." He pressed his nose tight against the glass. "Four more. Look."

Kate grinned, amazed once again at his ability with numbers. His autism kept him from communicating in other ways, but ask how many of something he saw, and he got it right every time. "What colors are they?"

Peter hunched down in the seat, and the humming started again.

Kate's mother draped her arm across the edge of the front seat and glanced back. "How many brown ones, Pete?"

"Six." He kept his face toward the road and gently rocked in time to the tune he hummed.

Dad smiled at Kate's mom. "Don't worry, Nan. He's going to be happier once he's out in the country. It'll be so much better than being cooped up in that small house."

Kate reached over the backseat into the rear compartment and stroked the coat of their German shepherd. The dog licked her hand as though sensing her distress. "Rufus will be happy too." *Everyone will be happy but me.* "It feels like we've been in this car for days."

Her dad laughed. "It's only been six hours since we left, Kate. We'll be home in another five minutes."

"It's not home, Dad. I still don't see why you couldn't have gotten a job in Spokane so I could stay at my school. It's not fair that I had to leave halfway through the year. I know Grandpa Cooper left the farm to Mom, but I don't see why you couldn't sell it and not move."

Her mom quirked an eyebrow. "Things aren't selling well right now. Dad's been out of work for so long, we couldn't afford to stay in Spokane. We'll get back on our feet sooner by not having to make a house payment."

"Yeah, I know, and I'm glad it'll be easier. So does that mean I can get a horse?" Kate blurted the question even though she figured she knew the answer. "I know, no horse. You have to pay for a special teacher for Pete."

"That's something he needs." Her mother's voice was soft but firm. "And a horse is the least of the expense. We'd need tack, feed, shoes, and so much more."

"But I *need* a horse. At least let me take lessons. If we'd stayed in Spokane, I could have kept working at the stables and taking lessons."

Dad slowed the car and turned on his blinker. "Let's talk about this later, all right? We're here."

Kate got her first glimpse of the farm in years and gasped. Because Grandpa had moved to assisted living when she was seven years old, she could barely remember this place. Hope filled her heart as she took in the wood-sided structure that seemed to go on forever. A barn. No, from the huge size, it more closely resembled a boarding stable or indoor arena. She barely glanced at the two-story farm house covered with peeling white paint. Getting inside that barn was all that mattered. White-washed wood fences surrounded three large paddocks, and pasture stretched out beyond. She shut her eyes, envisioning lush, green grass sprouting in another month or so.

When the car stopped, she swung open the back door and stepped out—right into a shallow puddle. "Dad! You parked in the mud." She kicked the toe of a sneaker against the back tire. "Gross."

"Sorry, Kate. Get Rufus out, okay? I'll grab our bags."

Kate walked around the car, opened the rear door, and grabbed her dog's collar. "Rufus, you big goof. Quit licking Pete's face." The shepherd landed beside her, and she motioned to her younger brother. "Time to get out, Pete. But watch where you step."

Kate moved to the open side door and extended her hand, but her brother didn't move. He continued to rock, hum, and stare out the opposite window. Worry pricked Kate's heart. She hated seeing Pete upset—it didn't seem fair. "Mom?"

Her mother stepped close and touched Pete's chin. He didn't pull back, but Kate saw him flinch. "Come on, honey." Mom waited patiently until Pete swung his legs out, but the humming continued.

Dad stretched his arms to the sky and rotated his head. "Feels good." Then he reached inside the rear compartment and grabbed two small overnight cases. "You kids ready to see the house? Pete's never seen it, and I'm not sure how much you remember, Kate."

She shook her head. "Who cares about a house when there's a barn and corrals? You didn't tell me the barn was so big, Mom. There's tons of room for a horse."

Her father ruffled her hair. "I'm afraid you're going to be disappointed, sweetie. You can look inside, but watch your step. There's a lot of junk in there, odds and ends, and thousands of cobwebs. The barn's only been used for storage for years."

"I'm not worried about a few spiders or junk." She patted her leg, and the shepherd bounded over, almost knocking her down in his excitement. "I'll take Rufus."

Dad nodded. "Be careful. He doesn't know this is his new home yet, and we don't want him running away."

Kate brushed a lock from her face, pulled off her scrunchie, then swept her brown, curly hair into a ponytail again. "Okay. Come on, Rufus. Stay close." She smiled at her family. Nothing about a barn could disappoint her. Just having one felt like a miracle. After all, barns were for horses, and she'd wanted a horse of her own *forever*.

Dodging another puddle, she headed toward the barn. She'd hated leaving her friends in Spokane and had worked hard to keep from resenting her parents for moving their family, but this discovery might very well make up for it—at least a little bit.

She opened the door, and the rusty hinges squealed as though saying she was entering a new world. It was going to be an awesome adventure—she could barely wait to get started!

Kate stared into the semidarkness and waited for her eyes to adjust to the dust-laden light filtering through the small windows high up on the walls. The barn had potential, and the large, empty space filled her head with ideas. The best one she could come up with: She'd meet a girl here who loved horses as much as she did … a girl with a sense of adventure. Together they would transform this place into an elegant riding stable. For the gazillionth time Kate wished Pete could share her excitement at a new discovery. What fun it would be to share this place with her brother and explore it together.

Her excitement dimmed a little as she peered through the gloom. What a mess! The metal bars set in the upper half of the stall doors were thick with cobwebs. Dust and grime clung to every surface, and the stalls had been used as a dumping ground for broken-down items too numerous to count.

She grabbed the bars of a stall and looked inside—an old bike with flat tires, a stack of oil cans, a rusty wheelbarrow, and a grubby easy chair that appeared to have been gnawed by rats. She shuddered and glanced at her feet. If that chair was an indication, there must be a lot of mice living in this place. *Mice and not rats*, she hoped. Even the windows were covered with dirt. Mom had said something about Grandpa liking to collect stuff, but this was crazy.

Kate kicked a flattened can out of her way and wandered to the end of the alleyway that fronted six stalls, with the indoor arena just beyond a half gate. At least the alleyway and indoor arena were empty. She peered across the wide arena, wishing the overhead lights were on. They were all probably burned out, since it didn't seem like anyone had cared for this barn in a long time. From what she could see, there were another four stalls on the other side of the arena and a closed door leading into some kind of room.

Kate swung open the half gate and jogged across the packed dirt. *One good thing*, she thought. *It's been so many years since horses were here, I don't have to worry about stepping in anything unpleasant.*

The gate on the far side was open, and Kate headed across the alleyway into a room that didn't look like a stall. "Cool!"

Rushing forward, she gazed at the dirt-encrusted English bridle hanging on a wood peg. She blew on it, then sneezed. "Dumb idea, Kate."

Spotting a box of rags in the corner behind an old metal desk and chair, she grabbed the cleanest one and wiped the bridle until leather showed through. "Awesome." She breathed the word, hardly believing her luck.

Now all she needed was the saddle and a horse to go with it.

Chapter Two

Four days later

Kate stood at the door to Odell Middle School, wishing she'd accepted her mother's offer to go with her the first day. Squaring her shoulders and shifting her backpack to her left arm, she grabbed the door and swung it open. She was almost thirteen, for goodness' sake, and not a baby, so she'd better quit acting like one. Thankfully Mom had come over on Friday afternoon to get her enrolled. Too bad Dad had gone to work that day, and Kate had to stay home and watch Pete. It might have made things easier if she could have come along and seen the school ahead of time.

She heaved a sigh of relief. At least she wasn't late. Dad had insisted on dropping her off, but tonight she'd ride the bus home. She'd rather walk, since it wasn't that far, but Mom didn't want her to the first couple of days. Kate had seen pastures loaded with horses between here and home. It would be fun to stop and see if one would come to the fence.

Locker doors slammed and kids gathered in clusters, laughing and clowning around, reminding Kate of her middle school back home. If only she were there with her friends and not in a strange place. Odell Middle School was so much smaller than she was used to—only one story, and it didn't even cover a city block.

The area had one thing going for it—the horses she'd seen. Maybe she could get on the Internet and see if there were any riding stables nearby. *If* they ever got the Internet hooked up at home. Maybe the library would have a computer she could use on her lunch break.

A couple of feet inside the door, Kate halted next to a high counter separating the entryway from the office and leaned her elbows on the hard surface. Long seconds passed, but no one looked her way. She cleared her throat with no results. "Excuse me?"

A young woman swung toward her and stared before a smile softened her plain features. "I'm sorry. With all the noise in the hallway, I didn't hear you. How can I help?"

The next several minutes were a muddle as Kate studied a school map and listened as Miss Thompson pointed her in the direction of her first class, math. Kate headed down the hall, glancing at the number above each door until she came to the right one. The bell for class sounded as she reached for the knob.

Her palms grew damp, and she wiped them against her jeans. What would her teacher be like? Back home she'd hated math. She'd never understood how to work her way through a story problem, and algebra baffled her completely. Her teacher had scowled every time he handed back one of her tests. Kate would much rather have classes that taught horsemanship or how to run a barn—now that would be practical. She'd certainly get an A in those.

Kate cracked the door and peered inside. Twenty pairs of eyes swiveled in her direction, and the teacher's speech came to an abrupt halt. Kate almost let go of the knob and backpedaled for home.

Thirty minutes had passed. Nothing terrible had happened, except for the teacher embarrassing Kate by telling her to introduce herself. The kids had all stared for a couple of seconds before Mr. Kyle rapped on his desk for order and returned to his topic. Thankfully he wasn't covering algebra or story problems today.

No notes or whispers were making the rounds, and the teacher hadn't picked on her once. Maybe this school wouldn't be as bad as she'd expected. One thing surprised her, though. She'd never seen so many Hispanic kids in a class. Her school back home had a multicultural population, but nothing like this. In fact, she'd counted, and there were more Hispanic students in this class than white. She'd never been the minority before, and it felt weird.

Kate hadn't realized she'd been staring at a petite, olive-skinned girl across the aisle until the girl turned and glared. *Oops.* Definitely not the way to make friends. She averted her gaze and prayed the bell would end this class before she did anything else wrong. Another girl stood out in the sea of black and brunette hair—a blonde sitting two rows ahead who tossed her hair and made eyes at the boy across the aisle. That girl probably thought she was pretty and liked to flaunt it, even though she didn't look all that hot to Kate. Someone else to stay away from.

The bell sounded as Mr. Kyle gave a homework assignment from the next chapter. Kate flipped to it and groaned. *Story problems. Ugh. But how many did he say they needed to do?* She stuffed her book under her arm and pivoted toward the front of the class. "Umph." She rocked back on her heels at the impact of a body against hers.

The dark-haired girl stepped around her. She wasn't exactly scowling, but she didn't seem happy either. She gestured toward the door. "We exit that way."

"Sorry. I was going to ask Mr. Kyle a question, but he's busy."

Another Hispanic girl pushed her way past and smirked as she bumped shoulders with her classmate. "Don't have enough of your own friends, Tori?"

The girl called Tori glanced at Kate and shrugged. "I can take care of myself, Mia."

Mia tossed her dark hair. "I hope so." She pivoted and headed toward the door but paused long enough to whisper something to another girl, who looked back at Kate and giggled.

Kate bit her lip to keep it from trembling. She'd better get to her next class, or she'd be late. She removed the schedule from her math book and tried to see it through the moisture blurring her eyes. All she wanted right now was to go home and never come back. She blinked hard, trying to clear her vision. It was no use. She'd probably never find her English class on time. She glanced toward the front of the room. Mr. Kyle was still talking to someone. Ramming the paper into her back pocket, she headed for the door.

She stepped out of the classroom and scanned both directions.

"You headed for English Lit?" Tori stood a few feet away, clutching her books.

Kate stopped, her heart hammering so loudly she was certain the petite girl would hear it. "Yeah, I guess so. If I can find it."

A tiny smile quirked one corner of Tori's mouth. "If we hurry, we can make it before the bell goes off. It's only two doors down the hall."

Maybe there was hope of making a friend after all. Kate followed Tori to the classroom and slipped in after her, then halted as the other girl found her seat in an area with no other empty desks. Kate glanced around, but no one seemed to care about the new girl. She lifted her chin, determined not to show hurt or confusion, and made her way to the front of the room to the one vacant seat. Her heart sank as the blonde girl sitting directly across the aisle shot her a condescending eye roll.

Kate slumped into the desk chair. Going back to Spokane sounded awfully good right now.

Chapter Three

Kate had never been so thankful for a day to end. Three days at this school, and she had yet to make a friend. She'd hoped it might happen after Tori offered to walk her to English Lit, but the girl hadn't spoken to her again. As Kate had settled into her seat in each new class, she felt a couple dozen pairs of eyes boring into her skull.

After buttoning her coat up to her neck and tugging on her gloves, she stepped out the front door of the school. What she wouldn't give right now for Mom to homeschool her. Thankfully her parents had agreed to let her walk home today, since it was only a little under a mile, and she knew the way. The days were getting longer, and it wouldn't be dark for another three hours, so she had plenty of time to get home.

Mom had also said it would be all right for her to stop and check out some of the horses along the way. Joy bubbled inside. She might not have a friend yet, but she was going to spend the next hour doing what she loved—making friends with her favorite four-legged creatures.

Striking out across the parking lot, Kate headed toward home. The new house didn't really feel like home yet, but she'd spent the daylight hours after school exploring the big barn and picking up the loose cans and bottles littering the ground. If she kept at it, maybe Dad would take a load of junk to the dump so one stall would be empty.

She'd discovered a pile of sawdust outside under a ragged tarp. The sawdust was mostly broken down and starting to turn to dirt, but she'd found enough that was still good to cover the floor of a stall. Somehow she'd find a way to convince her parents to buy her a horse of her own. Her birthday was next month, and they knew how much she wanted one. Now that Dad had a good job, maybe it would happen this year.

At that thought, she felt as though her feet had sprouted wings, and she flew across the road. Three bay horses lined the board fence about a half block away, their heads stuck over the top slat. Kate was thankful she'd tucked a bag of carrots into her backpack this morning. *Thoroughbreds, I think.* All of them were tall—maybe sixteen hands or better.

Kate slowed her pace and unzipped her backpack. She moved cautiously toward them, not wanting to spook them into taking off across the field. Withdrawing a carrot from a bag, she crept forward, the treat on the flat of her palm extended in front of her. One of the horses nickered and stretched his neck, nostrils flaring. Kate barely contained her joy when the big gelding's lips touched her palm as he latched on to the carrot.

"What are you doing?" a voice demanded from behind her.

Kate spun, nearly dropping her backpack, and placed her hand over her thudding heart. Tori stood a few feet away, her face twisted in amusement.

Whew. For a minute there, I thought I was busted by the owner and was going to get yelled at. "Feeding the horses carrots. Want to give them one?" Kate dug into the bag again, retrieved a long carrot, then broke it in half and held it out to the girl. "Horses love them."

Tori rolled her eyes. "I know that. Just because I'm Mexican doesn't mean I'm stupid."

Kate's cheeks warmed. "I'm sorry. That's not what I meant." She lowered her arm and wrapped her fingers around the carrots. "Guess I'd better head home."

"Wait." Tori stepped closer and held out her hand. " I didn't mean to be rude. I'd like to feed one if you promise the horse won't bite me."

Kate grinned. "I'll show you how. Keep your hand flat and don't curl your fingers up, and they'll snatch it without any problem." She demonstrated with one of the pieces.

Tori giggled as the bay gelding snuffed at Kate's hair after he'd munched his treat. "I think he wants more, and so do those other ones."

"Yeah. I brought a bunch." She broke several more into pieces and gave them to Tori. "My name is Kate."

Tori nodded. "I know." She peeked sideways at Kate, watching one more time as Kate fed a different horse. "Should I try now?"

"Sure. Give one to that bay mare." Kate indicated which horse with a nod. "I haven't fed her yet." She watched as Tori carefully extended her palm, keeping it flat. "Way to go! You did great!"

Tori held out another piece. "Thanks for sharing. She's pretty, and I didn't get bit." She kept her gaze on the horse. "I'm sorry about the way Mia treated you the other day. Not all of the kids here are like her."

Kate shrugged. "It's okay. It *was* kind of weird, though." She could have bitten her tongue after she'd blurted the words, and she prayed Tori wouldn't notice.

Tori stared. "What was?"

Kate groaned. "I didn't mean to say that."

"So explain."

"I'm not sure how. I guess it's weird for someone to act like they don't like me because of my skin color."

"Yeah, I don't especially like it either. But it's happened to me ever since I was little. I'm guessing this is your first time, right?" Her mouth twisted to the side.

Kate nodded, not sure what to say. She wished she'd kept quiet. The last thing she wanted was to make this girl mad when she might have finally found a friend.

Tori's face softened. "Don't let it bug you. I guess there are rude people in all races."

Relief hit Kate so hard, her legs wobbled. "Yeah. Thanks."

"So where do you live, anyway?" Tori motioned up the road and stepped away from the horses still reaching for treats. "I'm in that house across this pasture. The little yellow one. See it?"

Kate peered in the direction she pointed but only saw a building a little bigger than a shack. On closer inspection she noted that the windows had curtains and a tiny covered porch extended out front. "You have a big yard."

Tori nodded. "My dad's a gardener when he's not working at the packing plant. He loves flowers. And my mom puts in a huge vegetable garden in the summer."

Kate wrinkled her nose. "You mean a meat-packing plant?"

"No, silly, fruit. Haven't you noticed all the orchards between here and Hood River? In a few weeks, the cherry trees will start blossoming, and then the apples and other fruit. My dad's second job is yard work."

"Oh, right." Kate felt kind of dumb that she hadn't understood, but Spokane didn't have all the orchards that Odell and Hood River did. "I live that direction too. About a quarter mile on past you, I think. Want to walk together?"

"Sure." Tori waited for Kate to settle her backpack in place and then started off. "Do you have a horse? You know a lot about them."

Kate smiled. "I wish. I want one more than anything. We live on a farm and have a big, old horse barn that's dirty and needs work, but no horses came with it."

"So why'd you move to a farm, then?" Tori kicked at a rock on the edge of the pavement, sending it skittering across the road. A car zipped by seconds after, and the girls moved farther onto the grassy area along the shoulder.

"My Grandpa Cooper died several months ago and left my mom his farm. We lived in Spokane all my life, but my dad lost his job last year. When all the paperwork on the farm got finished, Mom and Dad decided we should move here. He started applying for jobs and found one." She stopped right before she admitted she wished they'd never moved. Maybe, with one friend on the horizon, she didn't feel that way as much as she had a few days ago.

Tori glanced at her. "Did you have a lot of friends in Spokane?"

Kate nodded. "Uh-huh."

"That's rotten you had to leave."

"Yeah."

Silence fell as they neared Tori's house. Kate was surprised how tidy everything was and felt ashamed of her earlier thought. Just because the house was small didn't mean it wouldn't be clean or nice. The windows glittered in the early spring sun, a tree swing hung from the limb of a giant oak, and an older-model pickup with gleaming paint was parked in the gravel drive. "Your house is bigger than it looked from a distance."

"Yeah. It's a three-bedroom, but two of them are tiny," Tori explained. "My little sister and I share, and my younger brother gets one of his own. *So* not fair."

Kate giggled. "I hear you. Maybe you can come to my house sometime? If you want to, that is." She waited, barely daring to breathe. "If you think your parents would let you, and you won't get in trouble with your other friends."

Tori didn't respond for a long moment, but then her eyes smiled. "My mom will want to meet your mom first, but if my friends have a problem with it, that's their deal, not mine."

"Cool!" Maybe living here wouldn't be so bad after all. If God had answered her prayer and sent her a new friend, maybe He'd be willing to send her a horse too.

Chapter Four

Spring was right around the corner—Kate could feel it—and so was her birthday. Only another week and the possibility she'd finally get her dream. She sucked in a shallow breath as she and Tori hiked across the parking lot at the end of the school day. "I'm glad it's Friday. I thought the week would never end."

Tori nodded and kicked a pebble across the asphalt. "Yeah, no kidding. That math test was brutal." She shuddered. "I sure hope I pass, or my dad isn't going to be happy."

Kate scrunched her face. "Your dad isn't mean, is he?" Her own father was one of the kindest men she knew, although his Marine Corps training still showed up at times. But he'd never hurt her or scared her like she'd heard some kids' dads did. As far as she was concerned, he was the best dad in the world.

Tori shook her head. "Nothing like that. He's cool. But he gets awful disappointed if I don't do well. He came to the US when he was seventeen and had to learn the language and find work. He married Mom a few years later, and he's always wished he could have done more with his life than work in the fruit-processing plant or spend his free time gardening. He and Mom want me and my brother and sister to go to college, but I've got to get good grades. There's no way I can go unless I get scholarships."

"You're smart. I bet you'll get lots of them when you're older." Kate hadn't even thought that far into the future. She had no real idea what she wanted to do after high school. Right now, making it through middle school seemed like enough. She hitched her backpack around and settled it more securely on her shoulders. "I don't even want to think about school this weekend. Want to go feed the horses again?" They'd made it somewhat of a ritual the past two weeks, and the horses were almost always waiting at the fence.

"I found a horse that I want you to see."

Kate swiveled and walked backward, keeping her eyes on Tori's face. "What do you mean, you found a horse? Not one we've been feeding?"

"Nope. This one's all by itself in a smaller pasture, and I think she's kinda sad and maybe hungry. I thought we could give our carrots to her this time."

Kate stopped and clutched Tori's wrist. "How far is it? Poor thing. I hope she's not starving. So it's a mare, not a gelding?"

Tori shrugged. "I didn't look to be sure. I still feel funny trying to figure it out, even after you showed me. But it has such a pretty face, I figured it has to be a girl."

Kate giggled. "I know what you mean. Come on, show me!"

Tori turned the corner and launched out across a field dotted along the edges with wild purple crocuses. "Be careful, there's an irrigation ditch not far ahead. You'll wreck your shoes if you fall in."

The girls jumped the ditch, shrieking and laughing, then raced across the weed-infested pasture. Tori slowed as she made her way down a narrow gravel road. After covering a block or so, she halted.

"There she is." Tori pointed toward a ramshackle, three-sided lean-to enclosed in a small paddock behind a single-story house. The open side of the lean-to faced the road, and a chestnut horse stood in the opening. The sun grazed her thick, dull coat as she poked her head outside.

Kate placed her hands on top of the three-rail fence that surrounded an area as big as Tori's house and yard but was completely bare of grass, except along the edges. "She's eaten everything down to the dirt, and I don't see any signs of hay."

"She's pretty woolly, and her mane is a tangle of knots." Tori leaned over the rail, peering at the horse.

"Yeah. It's early for her to shed out yet, but I can see her ribs even under that thick coat." Kate placed her backpack on the middle rail and unzipped it. After grabbing the bag of carrots, she tossed the backpack on the short grass behind her. It looked like the horse had stuck her head through the rails and grazed as far as she could reach. "Come here, girl—if you are a girl, that is," Kate crooned. She placed a carrot on her palm and extended it over the top rail. "I'll bet you're hungry. Want a treat?"

The horse snuffed the air, her nostrils flaring, but didn't budge from her station.

"What's wrong with her?" Tori took another carrot out of the bag where Kate had placed it and held the carrot out. "She's not sick, is she?"

"She doesn't know us. She's probably a little skittish. Give her time to get used to us. Talk soft and don't make any sudden moves. I think she'll come around."

They waited in silence, palms extended. Kate barely dared to breathe. Finally the mare dropped her head a little and inched forward. One step. Two. She halted and raised her head again, her eyes wide.

Kate smiled. "I don't think she's been handled in a while, but she wants to trust us."

Tori giggled. "Or she wants the carrots."

Kate grinned. "That too. Look."

The horse edged closer and stretched her neck to its limit. Her lips twitched, and then she took another step and snatched the carrot from Kate's palm and retreated. Munching so fast that Kate feared she would choke, the mare then moved toward Tori and snaked out her neck.

Kate kept her arm extended through the bars and slipped next to Tori. As the horse stretched for the last carrot, Kate stretched a little farther and stroked the furry neck. The horse skittered sideways but quickly returned and grabbed the treat.

Tori turned a glowing face to Kate. "Cool! She's not running away." Her words came out in a whisper. "Got any more carrots?"

Kate plucked the bag from the ground and emptied it into her and Tori's hands. This time the mare didn't hesitate but moved forward as soon as they reached through the bars.

Tori rubbed her damp hands on her jeans. "I wonder who owns her."

Kate stroked the mare's face as she continued to sniff their arms for more carrots. "You don't know who lives at that house?" She tipped her head toward the building on the far side of the lean-to.

"Nope. No curtains at the windows and no car in the driveway either. Maybe nobody lives here."

Kate frowned and ran her fingers down the mare's narrow white blaze, rubbing the soft hair under her forelock. "Do you think someone abandoned her?"

"I don't know, but we should ask around. My dad might be able to find out who owns the place. He knows a lot of people in Odell."

"Perfect. If someone dumped her off and isn't taking care of her, maybe I can talk my parents into letting me take her home."

Kate hung her head and fought back the tears threatening to tumble from her eyes. After a minute, she lifted her chin and stared at her dad. "Would you at least try to find out who the horse belongs to?" Right now, the last thing she wanted to do was finish clearing the dishes from the dinner table like she'd been told.

He tucked a strand of hair behind her ear. "I'm sorry, honey. I can ask around and hope we can help find a way to rescue the horse, but we're not in a position yet to buy you one. I've only been on this new job a couple of weeks, and it's going to take time for us to catch up."

"But I thought maybe for my birthday ..." Kate hated that her voice cracked on the last word. She shouldn't even have mentioned her birthday. The reminder would only make her parents feel worse than they did now. She could tell from Mom's sad eyes and Dad's worried expression that they wished they could do more. What had happened to their family wasn't their fault, but that didn't make it hurt any less. She'd set her heart on finding out if that mare had been abandoned and trying to adopt her. "But what if she's free? Maybe nobody wants her."

Pete started to hum, and Kate winced. She shouldn't have said that about nobody wanting the horse. Things like that often set Pete off. She stepped close to her little brother and lightly placed her arm around his shoulder, careful not to hug him tight. "Don't worry, Pete. Everything's okay."

He didn't pull away. A good sign. And the rocking didn't start. Kate sighed and took the last load of dirty dishes to the countertop next to the dishwasher.

Mom set a mug of coffee on the kitchen table and sank into a chair. "Thanks, Kate. I know you want a horse, and you're excited about the mare you and Tori found, but an animal like that isn't going to be free. Even if she was, there's still a saddle, the feed, hoof care, shots, and everything else that comes with properly caring for a horse. Maybe when you get older and can work part-time to help out ..."

Kate wilted. "At least we need to find out who owns her and make sure she gets fed. We can't let her starve. If nobody cares about her, she could die."

Dad nodded. "I'll ask around and see what I can find out. I wish we could get you a horse of your own, Kate. I'm not saying it won't happen sometime, but not until money isn't so tight. I'm sorry."

Kate straightened as hope returned. "Then I'll find a job." She smacked her forehead with the heel of her hand. "Why didn't I think of that before?"

Her dad glanced at her mother, who barely moved her head to the side. Dad cleared his throat. "You can't get hired at a real job until you have a work permit, Kate, and that's not until you're fifteen."

"I could babysit. Kids my age do that all the time."

"We'd have to check into that. You're still twelve, and I think you have to be older before you can legally care for a younger child who isn't your brother or sister."

"I'll be thirteen in a few days." She crossed her arms over her chest and tried to keep the frustration from brimming over into her voice, but it was *so* not easy. Yet if she'd learned one thing in her almost thirteen years, it was that her parents expected respect. Especially if she hoped to get what she wanted. A twinge of guilt pricked. *That might not be a great reason for treating them with respect.* But with the frustration she was feeling right now, it was the best she could do.

Pete began rocking in his chair, and the humming increased in intensity. She'd upset him again. He was so sensitive to everyone's emotions. For the hundredth time, Kate wished her little brother could communicate like other kids his age.

Mom held out her hand to Pete. "Come on. Let's go in the living room and read a story. Kate's fine, Pete. She just needs to talk to Dad for a bit."

Pete pushed back his chair but didn't take Mom's hand as they left the room.

Kate settled into the chair Pete had left. "I didn't mean to upset him, Dad."

"I know. It's not always easy having a little brother who's autistic." Dad leaned over and gave her a quick hug. Then he walked to the cupboard, took down a mug, and poured himself a cup of coffee.

"It's not easy for any of us, but I still love him." Kate didn't know why she felt so defensive. It wasn't like Dad had said anything wrong.

"Sure, we all do. But it's hard seeing him struggle and not be able to let us know how he's feeling other than humming or rocking or speaking an occasional sentence."

"He'll get better when he's older, won't he?" Kate clenched her fingers until the nails bit into her palms.

"The doctor thinks so. He's young, and he's made a lot of progress since he was diagnosed. He's talking more now than he was a year ago. Therapy helps a lot." He winced. "I'm sorry most of our extra money has to pay for that, and you don't get the special things you want. I'm sure it doesn't seem fair."

Once again tears stung Kate's eyes, but this time it was due to shame, not frustration or anger. "I guess it doesn't sometimes, but then I think about what it would be like if I'd been born with autism instead of Pete, and I realize how lucky I am. Then I feel rotten for complaining about not getting a horse."

"Have I told you lately how proud I am that you're my daughter?" Dad drew her to her feet and wrapped her in a bear hug.

She snuggled close for a minute before pushing away, embarrassed. "I'm getting too old for that, aren't I?" She grinned up at him.

"Not in my book, you aren't. Tell you what. I'll put some thought into how we can get you back into the horse world here in Odell." He held up his hand when she opened her mouth in excitement. "That doesn't mean getting your own horse, but maybe we can work something out. Give me a few days, okay?"

Kate tried to smile. Dad meant well, but she couldn't think of anything that would be nearly as good as getting that mare. She'd fallen in love the moment the horse took the first carrot out of her hand. "Sure, Dad. Whatever. Guess I'd better finish the dishes."

He didn't reply further but headed toward the living room.

As Kate watched him go, all her earlier thankfulness at being born without the problems her brother had trickled away. She wasn't going to give up. Even if she didn't get a horse for her birthday, she'd figure out a way to fulfill her dreams one way or another.

Chapter Five

Kate and Tori raced across the soggy front lawn, each intent on getting to the house first. Kate vaulted onto the front porch. "All right! I won!" She pumped her fist in the air as her friend skidded to a halt beside her.

Tori glared at Kate's legs. "Not fair. You're at least two inches taller than me, and I swear most of it is in your legs. You need to run track. I bet you'd beat everybody."

Kate shook her head. "I might have long legs, but I don't have the heart to sprint around a track and try to win a race. The only track I'm interested in is a show arena."

"Huh?"

Kate punched Tori lightly on the arm. "Horses, you goof. You know, showing? Jumping?"

At Tori's blank expression, Kate stopped. "What? You've never gone to a horse show? Ever?" She opened the front door and waved Tori in first.

"Nope. My parents aren't exactly rich, you know. And I've never hung around anyone who loves horses as much as you do. I've never even ridden on a horse."

"Whoa! No way!" Kate stared at Tori. "Never? I mean, I knew you weren't supercomfortable around them when you didn't know how to feed them carrots, but never?"

"N- E- V- E- R." Tori's chin firmed in determination. "And it never occurred to me to want to either. Clear now?"

"Sor-*ry*." Kate smirked, then sobered. "Really. I wasn't trying to make fun. I guess I've loved horses for as long as I can remember, so it's hard to imagine someone who didn't grow up wanting the same thing."

"Well, I didn't." Tori tossed her long, dark hair over her shoulder as she glanced back. "But now that you mention it, it might be fun. If it isn't a big horse and I don't get dumped. What's a horse show like? I've been to lots of football and basketball games at school, and my little brother's T-ball games."

Kate bit the inside of her cheek to keep from laughing. She'd already insulted Tori enough. The last thing she wanted was to hurt her friend's feelings. "Uh, it's nothing like any of those. Want to go with me? There's a big show here in Odell early this summer. I researched it on the Internet yesterday. It's a hunter-jumper show that's on the approved circuit."

"Huh?" Tori wrinkled her nose.

"Never mind. It just means if you place, you get points that accumulate along with points you earn from other shows. But the ad said the one here is outdoors in a field south of Odell, on the way to Hood River."

"Okay, sure. We better get in there. Your mom hollered that it was time for cake and presents ten minutes ago."

"Yikes!" Kate grabbed Tori's hand and sprinted for the dining room. "I almost forgot it's my birthday. Dad's going to eat all the cake if we don't get in there fast!"

Kate and Tori halted in the doorway of the dining room and gasped. Streamers and balloons exploded in color all over the ceiling and walls. A big sign colored in block letters and proclaiming HAPPY BIRTHDAY, KATE! hung above the far window. A cake shaped like a horse head sat in the center of the table, with thirteen candles running down the length of the mane.

"Awesome, Mom! Who made the cake? And when did you have time to decorate without me knowing?"

Mom chuckled and glanced at Dad. "I had a little help while Tori kept you busy outside. Pete even helped with the balloons, didn't you, buddy?"

Pete eyed all the various colors. "Thirteen balloons for Kate. Three yellow, two blue, two red, four pink, and two green."

Kate and Tori applauded. "Thanks, Pete! You did a great job."

He pointed to the left of the cake. "That's a horse. Now Kate has a horse."

Kate's heart stilled. "Yeah, it sure is. What are those next to the cake?" She waved her hand at the stack of presents, praying her little brother would keep talking.

He didn't meet her eyes or follow where she indicated but started to gently rock in his chair.

Dad patted her shoulder. "Don't worry, honey. He's fine. That was more than he usually says, and he's been in a happy mood the entire time we've been decorating. Do you want to open your presents first or cut the cake?"

She'd been staring at a big box behind three or four smaller items. "If everyone isn't dying to have cake first, I want to see what's in that box." She glanced around the room at the smiling faces. "In all of them, actually."

Mom pulled out a chair at the head of the table. "Take a seat, then, and let's get started. I'll admit to being pretty excited about that box myself."

Dad held his finger to his lips. "Nan, don't give her any hints."

"I'm not, John. But I can't wait to see what she thinks."

Kate dragged a chair close to the table and leaned forward. "Do I get to open it first?"

Tori twisted a strand of hair around one finger. "Uh, do you mind if you wait and leave it for last? I'm afraid you won't want to see mine after you open the big one."

"You know what it is?" Kate stared at her friend and then at her parents, who grinned back at her. "You do! Fine," she said with a dramatic flourish, "which one do you want me to open first?"

Tori grabbed a gift bag with a pink bow on the handle and thrust it under Kate's nose. "Mine. Please."

Kate laughed and grabbed the bag. "Want me to guess?"

"No, silly. And don't shake it, or it might break. Just open it."

Kate slit the tape that held the top closed and peeled back the heavy folds of tissue. "Oh, cool!" She withdrew a delicately molded horse figurine. "It's beautiful! And it looks like that mare we found last week. Where did you get it, Tori?"

Tori dropped her eyes, and a flush colored her dusky cheeks. "You're not supposed to ask questions like that."

Kate blinked, not sure what to think. Then, spotting a tiny chip on the base, she understood. Tori's family didn't have a lot of money, and any gift would be a sacrifice. Tori might have gotten it at a discount store or even a yard sale, but it didn't matter. "It's perfect. I absolutely *love* it! Thank you!"

Tori's warm brown eyes lit with joy. "I'm glad you like it. I was kind of worried."

"Silly. How could I not love it?" Kate tossed her friend a grin and then tore into the next two gifts—a box of her favorite chocolates from Pete and a small, framed horse print from her parents. Grandma and Grandpa Ferris had sent a gift certificate and a new T-shirt with a horse logo.

Now the oversize box sat alone on the table, and Kate's fingers itched to open it. Her family hadn't given her the slightest hint what it might be. It wasn't big enough to hold a horse, so she didn't have a clue. "Can I open it now?"

Mom nodded. Dad went around the corner, hefted it from where it sat, and placed it in front of Kate.

She stood and leaned over the box, rising on her toes and bouncing. Slowly she tore off a large strip of the pink polka-dot paper, only to reveal a regular cardboard box with no lettering or hint of what might be inside. With sudden resolve, Kate tore into the rest of the wrapping, removing it in a matter of seconds. She eyed the seam secured with what appeared to be an entire roll of tape, and spluttered, "Wow! Who sealed this thing, anyway?"

Her brother patted his chest. "Pete."

Kate's mouth gaped, and then she snapped it shut and swallowed. "Good job, buddy."

Dad handed her his pocketknife, and she slit the tape and grabbed the two flaps, popping the box apart. Still no clue. A ream of newspaper packed the entire top. She dug beneath it until her fingers touched something hard. She shoved the paper aside, grabbed hold of the item, and hoisted it up and out of the box.

"Awesome!" She squealed the word and almost dropped the present in her excitement. "An English saddle ... This is the best present ever!"

The smiles on her parents' faces almost lit the room. "We hoped it was the right type. The lady at the store in The Dalles said this should be the right size for your height and weight." Her mom's forehead crinkled. "I hope you don't mind that it's used. She said it's good quality, and all the fittings are there."

"No problem. A used saddle is already broken in. Now all I need is a horse to put it on." Kate lifted her eyes toward her parents, only to see the delight fade from their expressions. "I didn't mean it like that, you guys. I mean, this is perfect. Thank you *so* much!" She had no idea what she'd do with a saddle and no horse, but this gift only served to strengthen her determination. Somehow, someway, she'd get her wish.

Chapter Six

Kate ran from her bedroom and snatched the ringing phone from its cradle in their living room, wishing yet again that her parents would allow her to have her own cell phone. They didn't really have the extra money, and neither saw it as a necessity, but she felt so out of it at school. A lot of kids had their own phones and spent breaks or lunch texting or surfing the web. Maybe she'd put that on her Christmas list.

"Hello?"

"Hey, it's Tori."

"What's up?" Kate settled into the deep cushion of their sofa, still amazed that God had brought her a friend so soon after they'd moved here.

"You got anything planned today? Are you done with your chores?"

"Yep. Mom's working with Pete, and Dad ran to Hood River. I decided to stay home. What's going on?"

"Since it's not raining, I thought you'd like to go for a bike ride. My mom said it was okay, and there's something I want to show you."

Kate's ears perked. "Cool. I'll ask Mom, but I'm sure she won't care. Want to head over?"

"Yep. Be there in fifteen."

"Great. I'll be ready." Kate set the phone back in the cradle, happy she'd gotten her chores out of the way early and even more thankful it was Saturday. What could Tori want to show her? They'd been back to visit the mare a few more times during the week after her birthday, but no one seemed to know anything about who owned her or where she'd come from. Frustration nipped at Kate, but she pushed it away. No time to get grumpy now with Tori on the way and a secret adventure looming ... Well, she hoped it would be an adventure. She'd love a mystery to solve or for something exciting to happen.

Right on time Tori knocked on the door, and Kate rushed to answer it. "Mom said it's fine, but she doesn't want me gone more than a couple of hours. She also wants to know where we're going." Kate rolled her eyes. "You know how parents are."

Tori slumped. "Aww, I wanted it to be a surprise."

Kate's mom walked into the entry. "I thought I heard Tori's voice." She gave the girl a quick hug. "It's good to see you." She glanced from Kate to Tori. "So you'd like to keep your destination a surprise from Kate, is that what you mean?"

Tori nodded, and her dark brown ponytail bounced on her shoulders. "If that's okay, Mrs. Ferris."

Mom half turned toward the living room and pointed. "How about you follow me and whisper what you're doing. Then I'll know and Kate won't. Will that work?"

Tori's eyes shone. "Sure." She shot a look at Kate. "No eavesdropping."

Kate gave a mock salute. "Yes, ma'am!"

But when Tori and her mom started talking in low tones, Kate almost broke her word. She stopped herself in time from tiptoeing to the doorway. She didn't want to disappoint Tori or ruin her surprise. Even more than that, she didn't want to break her word to her new friend.

It felt like forever, but it was probably only a minute or two later when Tori reappeared. "Ready?"

"You got that right!" Kate wrenched the door open. "Lead me to it, girl."

Tori bounced down the porch stairs and grabbed her bike, wheeling it toward the gravel road fronting Kate's yard. "Hurry up, or I'll leave you behind."

"Fat chance of that!" Kate jumped aboard her own bike and pushed on the pedal, excitement making her catch her breath. "Which way are we going?"

"To the left, and that's all I'll tell you. Follow me, and you'll see soon enough."

They pumped up a slight rise, standing on their pedals to crest the top, and then coasting down the other side. It was harder work on gravel than it would have been on pavement, but Kate didn't mind. She'd discovered since moving here that she loved living in the country. It wasn't even as bad at school as she'd expected, now that she'd met Tori. Kids like Mia, the blonde girl Melissa, and several others still weren't friendly, but she hadn't been harassed or bullied like some kids she'd known at home. Not that she hadn't seen a little of that in her weeks at Odell, but overall most of the kids were decent.

Tori slowed her pace at the bottom of the decline and squinted over her shoulder. "You coming?"

Until Tori hollered, Kate hadn't realized that she'd slowed to a crawl to gaze out over the nearby field of horses. "Yeah. Sorry!" She pumped her legs to catch up. "Where to now? I love this ride. My favorite stable is up around the next bend. They've got some awesome horses."

Tori grinned but didn't reply, just jerked her chin forward and pedaled faster.

Kate dug in and increased her pace, dying to know where they were headed. Tori had never acted so mysterious. Before, Kate had been the one to suggest going for rides or visiting the mare they'd found, so this was kinda weird.

After they'd ridden over a mile from home, Tori slowed her bike at the gravel entrance to the large equestrian barn, and Kate skidded to a stop beside her. "Tori! What's going on? We're really going in here? This is too cool!" She brushed a loose strand of hair from her face. "I've been wanting to visit, but since I don't own a horse, I didn't think they'd let me. Do you know someone who has a horse boarded here?"

Tori planted both feet on the ground, straddling her bike. "I guess I'd better tell you now. I hope you aren't going to be upset with me. I'm not so sure this is a good idea now that we're here."

Kate stared at her, wondering if Tori had lost her mind. "Of course it's a good idea. It's great! Why would I get mad because we're at the coolest horse barn in the area?"

"I saw an ad in the paper that they need people to clean stalls."

Kate's heart skipped. "Awesome! I told Mom and Dad I want to get a job and save money for my own horse. This is perfect." Her joy faded as a new thought struck. "If you want to apply, I won't, Tori. You saw the ad, so I shouldn't butt in. I hope you'll be able to get the job."

Tori shook her head. "That's not the deal. They need more than one person, so you can apply too, but it's not a paying job. Well, it doesn't pay money. They'll let people work in exchange for board or lessons. Neither of us has a horse to board, but I was thinking, maybe …"

Kate pumped her fist in the air. "Lessons? Oh man, that's so cool! This is the best surprise ever." Then her smile faded. "But I can't put in an application without talking to my parents first."

Tori blew out a puff of air between her parted lips. "Whew. I'm glad you're excited about it. I started worrying on the way here that it was a really dumb idea. And don't worry about getting permission; I told your mom, and she said it was fine. It's close to home, so they wouldn't have to drive you. My parents said I could check it out, and your mom said the same thing. So we're good."

An hour later Kate and Tori rose from their seats at the metal desk in the barn office. "So you'll let us work here, Mrs. Wilder?" Kate glanced at the young woman who had pushed to her feet on the other side of the desk. Her blonde hair was gathered back into a knot at the base of her neck, and she wore riding breeches, tall boots, and a form-fitting knit shirt.

Mrs. Wilder nodded. "I think you girls will do fine. We haven't had a lot of applications yet, so it's good you got here right after the ad came out. We're agreed on two hours after school, two days a week, and two hours on Saturday in exchange for two hours of riding lessons each on one of our lesson horses?"

"Yes, ma'am." Both girls spoke at the same time.

Kate was so happy she could barely keep her grin from splitting her cheeks. "Since today is Saturday, did you want us to start now?" She looked down at her good sneakers and new jeans, wondering what her mom would say if she came home with stains on either one.

Mrs. Wilder must have read her thoughts. "No, you can start on Tuesday, come back on Thursday, and then plan on being here two hours on Saturday morning. Does that work for you both?"

The girls glanced at each other. "You bet," Kate replied as Tori nodded. "It's not even going to be hard to not sleep in on Saturday. I can't wait till Tuesday to get started."

"How about I show you around now so you'll be better acquainted and know what to do when you come?"

"Yeah." Kate breathed the word. "And could we see the horse we're going to take lessons on, please? If you have time?"

"Of course. Follow me." Mrs. Wilder led them along the alleyway running between the indoor arena and in front of the long row of stalls, pausing at each one to introduce the girls to the horse housed inside. "Most of the horses here belong to boarders, and you won't be handling any of them at first." She stopped at a stall that appeared empty and beckoned them forward. "This is Lulu, one of my personal favorites."

Kate and Tori looked at each other in confusion. Tori stepped a little closer to the bars. "I don't see anything, Mrs. Wilder."

The woman laughed and unlatched the door, then slid it to the side. "That's because Lulu is thirteen and a half hands tall. She's a POA. She's quite a bit taller than a Shetland but shorter than a full-size horse."

Kate moved to the opening to see a darling pony that resembled a perfectly formed Appaloosa, only smaller. She was mostly black but had a black-and-white blanket over her rump and a white strip running from under her forelock to the tip of her nose. "What's a POA?"

"Pony of the Americas, a breed developed in the 1950s from an Arabian, Appaloosa, and Shetland pony cross. They're gentle and easy to train and make wonderful lesson and show horses for kids."

Kate's heart sank. She'd assumed they'd get to ride a full-grown horse, maybe a Thoroughbred or Warmblood, but a pony? Sure, she was cute and all, but this wasn't what she'd expected. "So … Tori and I will take lessons on Lulu instead of a regular horse?"

"That's right," Mrs. Wilder acknowledged. "And don't worry, she won't disappoint you. Lulu knows everything there is to know about hunt-seat, pulling a cart, showing at halter, and even riding Western. You both said you're pretty much beginners, and I want to start you slow and make sure you get a good foundation before you move to something bigger. Does that make sense?"

Kate cast a glance at Tori, who nodded. "Sure. I guess so. Lulu is awful cute, but I did take several lessons in Spokane."

"We'll see how you do during your first two or three lessons and then decide. She'll be your responsibility on the days you work here. You'll need to clean her stall, bed it with fresh shavings, feed her hay and grain on Saturday, groom her, and check her feet. One of our grooms will show you how to do all of that Saturday morning. We'll have you clean stalls for other horses, too, but you won't groom any of them until we're sure you're comfortable and know what you're doing."

Tori edged forward and stroked the little mare's face. "How long do we need to work before we get our first lesson?"

"How about next Saturday after you finish your chores?"

Kate ran her hand along Lulu's neck, surprised that the pony seemed to have already shed most of her winter coat. *They must*

*blanket the horses through the winter to keep them from growing
too dense a coat*, she thought. The stable in Spokane did that
during the coldest part of the winter. Kate was always glad, as it
seemed so cruel to allow the horses to stand outside and shiver.
She'd seen too many horses in deep snow, with no shelter and
icicles hanging from their manes, not to appreciate a well-cared-
for animal. "I'd love to take my lesson that day, but I'll need to
check with my mom about how long we can stay."

Tori's mouth formed an O. Kate gave a quick nod, reading
her friend's mind.

Mrs. Wilder raised a brow. "I'm sorry, did I miss something?"

Kate hunched a shoulder. "Yeah. We both realized we
haven't asked our parents for sure about the work schedule. They
know we're here asking about a job in exchange for lessons, but
I guess we should okay it with them for sure before we come on
Tuesday."

Tori twisted a strand of hair around her finger, her eyes wide
and pleading. "Does that mean you'll give our jobs to other
people because we can't tell you yes right now?"

Mrs. Wilder hesitated. "Do you think you could both let me
know by this evening? I'll give you my business card, and you
can call my cell. Will that work?"

Kate's breath whooshed out. "That would be awesome.
Thank you! We'll talk to our parents as soon as we get home."

They spent another ten minutes visiting the well-equipped tack room that contained saddles, bridles, halters, grooming tools, and other items Kate couldn't even identify. When they moved on to the wash rack for bathing the horses, Mrs. Wilder swiveled toward the girls. "I'm afraid that's all I have time for. If you call and say you can go to work next Tuesday, I'll be sure someone shows you the loft where we keep the hay, as well as explains how to properly clean the stalls, where to get clean sawdust, and how to dispose of the material you remove. I have a lesson coming up soon, so I need to go. I hope to hear from you both this evening. And remember, I want you girls to work as a team, so I really hope both of your parents will agree."

Kate and Tori thanked her and walked the length of the barn to the spot where they'd parked their bikes. Kate barely kept from bouncing the entire way through the barn, she was so ecstatic about this new opportunity. Lessons in exchange for a few hours of work. And it was work that she loved, hanging out in a big barn around amazing animals. It didn't get much better than this, and she had Tori to thank for it.

She climbed onto her bike and pushed it around in a half circle, then spotted Tori's face. Her lips were pinched together like she was trying not to cry. "What's the matter? Aren't you excited about this place? I can't believe we actually get to hang out here."

Tori brushed her hand over her eyes. "Yeah. I am."

"But?" Kate leaned closer, trying to get Tori's attention, but her friend kept her gaze averted. "Tori? What's up? Did you change your mind?"

"No. I want to do this more than anything. But I don't think my mom believed it would come to anything. She said I could take a bike ride and see what the ad was about, but she said not to get my hopes up about working here."

"Then she's going to be surprised when you come home and tell her you landed a job, right? She's not going to care, is she?"

Tori still didn't meet Kate's eyes. "She's terrified of horses and thinks they're dangerous. If she finds out I'll be handling a horse at all, much less riding one, I don't think she'll approve. I don't know why I didn't think this through before coming. I didn't realize we'd be grooming and handling horses on our own. I told Mom we might get a job cleaning stalls, and she seemed okay with that, but she might freak if she knows I'd be riding a horse."

"Oh man! I can't believe this!" The instant the words left Kate's mouth, she wished she could yank them back. Tori's face fell, and her eyes brimmed with tears. "Hey, Tori, I'm sorry. It's okay, really. We'll talk to your mom together, and I'm sure my mom will talk to her too. It'll work out, and if it doesn't …" She sucked in a deep breath, not sure she could squeeze the words out but knowing she had to. "If it doesn't, I won't take the job either. It's all or nothing. You're the one who saw the ad and brought me here, and I'm not doing this without you."

Tori raised her head. "But you want this even more than I do. It's not like I've always dreamed of owning a horse or taking lessons."

Tori's expression of amazement and gratitude pushed aside Kate's disappointment. "That's what friends are for. But we'll convince your mom that horses aren't dangerous, and she'll come around. Wait and see." Kate forced a smile and was relieved to see an answering one on Tori's face.

Inside, though, Kate felt sick. She'd given her word that she wouldn't take the job if Tori couldn't, and she'd keep it, because a friend was more important than a job.

But the thought of riding away from this place and maybe never coming back was almost more than Kate could bear.

Chapter Seven

Kate stood in the crowded living room at Tori's house and gnawed the inside of her cheek to keep the tears from falling. She couldn't believe what she'd heard. Then again, maybe she shouldn't be surprised, since Tori had warned her.

"But, Mom, nothing is going to happen to me. The people at the barn said they'd show us the right way to do everything. I won't get hurt."

Mrs. Velasquez folded her arms across her chest. "I said you could go talk to them, Victoria, but you shouldn't have said yes until you spoke to your papi and me."

Tori rocked on her toes, her jaw clenched. "We didn't exactly say yes; we said probably. Mrs. Wilder knows we have to clear it with our parents first."

"Good. Then there is nothing more to talk about."

"Mom! That's not fair. I'm going to be cleaning stalls and grooming horses that are tied up. What's so dangerous about that?"

"In exchange for lessons where you must ride a horse. Is that correct, Kate?" Her eyes swung toward Kate.

"Uh. Yes, ma'am. But it's not really a horse. Lulu's a pony." She held her hand out level with her chest to show the horse's height. "We'd be in an enclosed arena anytime we ride. With an instructor there."

"But you could get bucked off. Or kicked. Or stepped on by one of the horses you groom. Horses can hurt you, even if they are ponies."

Tori tipped her head back and closed her eyes for a second. "Even if I fell off, the ground is soft. They keep it tilled up so people won't get hurt. And like Kate said, the pony is short, so it's not far to fall. And if she stepped on my foot, she doesn't weigh enough to matter."

Mrs. Velasquez looked from Tori to Kate. "What do your parents say, Kate? Will they allow you to do this?"

Kate straightened her spine and mustered a smile. "I haven't asked them yet, but I'm pretty sure it will be all right. My mom was raised around horses when she was a kid, and they allowed me to take riding lessons in Spokane."

"Were you ever injured while taking lessons?" Tori's mother stepped a little closer. "Please be very honest with me."

"No. Never. Riding stables try to get gentle, tame horses for their students to use. Mrs. Wilder says the pony is well trained and sweet. I honestly don't think Tori would get hurt."

Mrs. Velasquez gave a slow nod and turned to Tori. "I won't say no without asking your papi first, and I'll think about what you've both told me, but no promises. Understood?"

Tori's shoulders sagged. "Yeah. Can I talk to Papi about it myself? Please?"

Her mother exhaled heavily. "I know what he'll say if you do. You let me talk to him. *Si?*"

"*Si.*"

"Now Kate needs to go home and ask her parents if she has permission. If she doesn't, then it won't matter what your papi says. You cannot work at that place by yourself."

"I don't want to without Kate, anyway."

"Good."

Kate edged toward the front door, anxious to leave the tension-filled home and talk to her parents. She'd assumed Mom and Dad would say yes, but now she was wondering. Had she gotten her hopes up for nothing? Somehow God had to make Mrs. Velasquez change her mind. She was going to pray all the way home. Maybe she could even get her mother to talk to Tori's mom. "I'd better get home, Tori. I'll call you later, okay?"

Tori nodded. "Yeah. Sure."

Kate hesitated, then whispered into Tori's ear, "I'm going to pray like crazy that your mom lets you go."

A small smile flitted across Tori's face as she stepped away. "Thanks. See you."

Kate lifted her hand as she walked toward the door, but the joy she'd felt while at the barn had disappeared.

"Please, God," she repeated on the bike ride home, "I want this so bad."

As she parked her bike in her front yard, another thought hit her. All the praying she'd done had been for herself, not Tori. She stopped in the yard and bowed her head as shame washed over her. "I'm sorry, Lord. Please do what's best for Tori and for me, and help us both not be too bummed if her parents still say no." She raised her head and peeked up at the sky. "But I'd sure appreciate it if You'd speak to her mother and take away her fear. Amen."

Kate sat by the phone, willing it to ring. She'd already called Tori and told her that Mom and Dad had said yes, as long as she kept up with her homework and chores. Tori's dad wasn't home yet, and Tori had promised to call as soon as he made a decision. Kate wasn't sure she could stand it much longer, but she'd been praying more than she'd prayed about anything for a long time.

The phone jangled and Kate jumped, even though she'd been waiting. She snatched it up. "Hello?"

"Kate? It's Tori." The words were flat, almost without expression.

Kate sucked in a quick breath before she replied. "They said no." It wasn't a question. Kate knew without asking that her dream had ended before it had begun, and Tori would never have the chance to ride a horse or know the freedom and joy of connecting with a big animal. Sadness washed over Kate.

"Yeah. I thought Papi was going to say yes, but then he looked at my mom and stopped." Tori sounded defeated.

"Maybe she'll change her mind. Did you try talking to your dad alone?"

"No. I could tell it wouldn't do any good. I'm sorry, Kate. I never should have taken you over there and gotten your hopes up. It's okay if you take the job without me."

For one wild second, hope flared in Kate's heart. She sucked in a breath and let it out slowly. "No way. I made a promise, and I'll keep it. We do it together or not at all."

"But that's not fair to you. Your parents said yes, so you should go. It's not like they'll hold the job for us very long."

Kate clutched the phone tight in her fist, knowing Tori was right but hating the idea of giving up so easily. "Yeah. I'll call Mrs. Wilder tonight and ask if she'll let us have through tomorrow to give her a decision."

"I'm not sure what good that will do, but I suppose it can't hurt—if she's willing to wait. Hey, I have to go. I'll let you know if anything changes." Her voice wavered on the last two words. "Thanks for being such a good friend, Kate."

Kate set the receiver down and sat without moving. She was glad she'd done the right thing, even if it was one of the hardest choices she'd made in her life.

She got up from the couch and headed toward her parents' bedroom. She found her mother curled up on the bed cradling Pete in one arm and holding a book—*Pete's Dragon*, her brother's all-time favorite.

Her mother lifted her eyes as Kate leaned against the door frame. "I heard the phone. Was it Tori?"

"Yeah."

"Not good news, I take it?" She shifted on the bed but kept her arm around Pete. Story time was one of the rare opportunities when her brother allowed physical contact, so Mom read to him whenever he asked.

"Tori's parents said she can't work at the barn. Her mother is afraid she'll get hurt taking care of the horses."

"That's too bad, honey. I know this meant a lot to you."

"I figured if I couldn't have my own horse, this was the next-best thing. Tori and I would work and take lessons together, and it would even be better than when I took lessons at home, 'cause I'd have a friend with me. I'm so bummed, Mom. It's not fair."

She frowned, not wanting her mother to see how much it hurt. It wasn't their fault they couldn't afford to get her a horse of her own or pay for private lessons that she didn't have to work for. At this point Kate would be thrilled with an occasional group lesson or even the chance to hang out at the barn and groom the horses. Anything but sitting at home every day after school. Summer vacation would start in about seven weeks, and she'd been so sure she and Tori would get to work all the way through, with both of them becoming excellent riders by the time summer ended.

Pete looked almost directly at Kate, his eyes wide. "Pete will get Kate a horse."

Chapter Eight

Kate straggled behind her parents out of the community church they'd started attending, wishing Tori had made it this morning. Kate had been thrilled when she discovered that Tori's family attended the same service, and she'd hoped her friend might come this morning with the news that her parents had changed their minds. Tori's father had come, but Tori and her mother hadn't shown up.

Dad stepped up beside her. "Want to ride home with your mother or walk with me?" Her father had a thing about keeping in shape and rode his bike or ran whenever he could. She forced a smile, not wanting to hurt his feelings by refusing. "I'll go with you if you promise not to run too fast. I'm not exactly wearing my running shoes."

He glanced at her feet and grinned. "I don't see how girls can walk in those stiff-soled things, but I came prepared." He drew his hand from behind his back, and her tennis shoes dangled from the tips of his fingers. "I was hoping you'd come with me. Mom and Pete will drive home so Mom can get lunch started."

A real smile tugged at her lips this time. *Leave it to Dad to think about grabbing my shoes.* "Good thing this church doesn't mind people wearing jeans on Sunday morning. If I'd been wearing a dress, I'd have to ride home with Mom."

He ruffled her hair, something he'd done since she was little, and she didn't have the heart to ask him to stop now that she was a teenager. Besides, a part of her still kind of liked it. He tugged on one of her loose curls and then tucked it behind her ear. "Slip into these shoes and give your mom your good pair. Then we'll hit the road."

Kate did as he asked, tossing her shoes into the backseat of the car, then leaning in through the front passenger window. "Don't eat all the food before I get home, Pete." She tweaked his nose.

He yanked away from her touch. "Pete's not a pig. Where's your horse, Kate?"

She wondered why he was stuck on this new theme. Sure, she'd talked a lot about the thin mare she and Tori had discovered and fed carrots to and had even taken Pete to visit the horse one time. It had to be because he'd heard her disappointment over not getting the job at the barn.

Sometimes she thought her little brother understood a lot more than he let on about the things going on around him. He was smart in so many ways. It was just trapped and bottled up inside, and he needed help letting it out. That's what it seemed like to her, anyway.

"No, kiddo. I don't have a horse yet, but maybe someday. How about you keep an eye out for one you think I'd like while you're riding in the car. Can you do that?"

Pete nodded, and then the humming started again. He slumped down in his seat, almost too short for the seat belt buckled around his thin frame.

Kate waved. "Love you, bud."

He didn't reply, just rocked and hummed and stared out the front window.

As the car pulled away, Kate moved back and almost bumped into her dad. She didn't even realize her cheeks were damp until he ran a thumb down her face and wiped one away.

"It's hard, isn't it, honey?"

She knew what he meant without asking. "It doesn't seem fair that he's trapped in his own world."

"But he's getting better. Remember a year ago when he barely spoke?"

She nodded. "Yeah. He's come close to looking at me a few times, and he even talks sometimes without me speaking to him first. I guess that's an improvement."

"It's huge, Kate. Keep praying for him. God loves Pete even more than we do."

Her heart jolted. She'd prayed so many times this weekend about getting her dream job and never once thought about praying for her little brother. That would change. "I will, Dad."

They struck off across the short parking area and reached the edge of the paved road. Dad increased his pace but didn't break into a run, and Kate was thankful. If it were up to her, she'd take her time all the way home. As much as she enjoyed spending time with her father, nothing much sounded good right now. Still, she ventured a try. "So, how's your new job?"

"It's a job. Not what I was hoping for, since my training is in aviation and business management, but hey, it pays the bills."

"That's good. I hate to see you guys worried about money."

Little ridges formed between her dad's eyes. "I'm sorry if your mom and I have made you worry."

"I'm not a baby anymore, Dad. I can handle it."

"I know you aren't, but that's not the point. We're the parents, and we should keep that kind of stress away from you kids." He took her arm and moved her farther onto the shoulder as an oversize pickup zoomed past, barely slowing or moving toward the center line. "Let's walk for a bit. I have something to tell you. I was going to wait until we got home, but your mother said I shouldn't."

Kate's mind skittered, trying to come up with whatever it might be. It didn't sound like she was in trouble, although he looked awfully serious. "Uh, did I do something wrong?"

"Nothing like that." He pressed his lips together. "Mom and I have been talking. We feel bad that you didn't get to take the job when it meant so much to you. We want you to know how proud we are that you stuck by Tori and didn't go to work without her."

Kate gaped at him. She hadn't said a word to either of her parents about not taking the job if Tori didn't get permission. "Thanks, Dad. But what do you mean about sticking by Tori? Did she say something to you about it?" That would be too weird, since Tori barely knew them. Kate couldn't imagine talking to Mr. or Mrs. Velasquez without Tori there.

"Not a thing. But like you say sometimes, we're not completely stupid." His huge grin took any sting from his words.

Kate laughed. "Yeah, and now that you're saying it back to me, I might not ever say that again."

"That works for me. Anyway, I'm guessing you could have had the job there if you wanted it, even if Tori didn't get permission. You showed her what true friendship looks like, and we think that's a pretty big deal. We're not rewarding that behavior, mind you, because it's reward enough that you did the right thing. However …"—he drew to a halt and touched her arm, bringing her to a stop beside him—"we know you're disappointed. I called the barn and talked to Mrs. Wilder. She's willing to hold a couple of part-time positions open for another day or two, in case. And besides that, we made arrangements with her for you to have three group lessons over the next six weeks. If Tori's parents don't change their minds, that is. I know it's not the private lessons you hoped for, but right now that's all—"

Kate threw her arms around her father. "That is *so* cool, Dad! Any kind of lessons will be awesome. I don't care if they're private. At least I'll be on a horse." She relaxed her hold and stepped back. "Ugh."

"What's wrong? I thought you were excited."

"I am. But Mrs. Wilder told me we'd have to take our lessons on Lulu, a pony."

"She mentioned that, but I told her you'd taken some lessons in Spokane. She said she'd only have you ride Lulu one or two times to judge your riding ability. Then, if you show you know what you're doing, she'll move you to one of the full-size horses."

Kate closed her eyes as happiness washed over her. "Nice. You and Mom are the best parents in the world."

He laughed and grabbed her hand, pulling her along beside him as he broke into a slow jog. "You think that now, but I hope you'll remember that the next time you get mad about something."

Kate huffed. "Whatever, Dad. But seriously, I appreciate it. I just wish Tori could come with me. It's so much more fun with a friend, and she's never even ridden a horse. I don't understand why her mom is so freaked about it. Can we go a little slower?"

Dad shortened his stride. "Has Tori asked her why? Maybe she has a good reason."

"I don't know. I suppose she could, but it seems weird to me. It's not like we're working at a rodeo and we're going to be riding wild horses or anything."

They finished the last ten-minute stretch in silence, but Kate didn't mind. It gave her time to think about what her father had said. It never occurred to her that Mrs. Velasquez might have a real reason for being afraid. Maybe she'd ask Tori the next time they talked. Kate and her dad walked the last couple of minutes and arrived at their front yard a half hour or so from when they'd left the church.

Dad opened the door and waited for her to enter. Then he followed her across the threshold, calling, "Anybody home? Where's my favorite wife and son?"

Kate giggled. "Dad, you only have one wife and son."

"And a good thing, or your mother would probably shoot me." He bumped her shoulder with his. "Something smells good in the kitchen. Let's go see what Mom has for lunch."

Kate traipsed behind her father, passing the comfortable living area and stopping in the doorway to the kitchen. "I'm starving."

Dad placed a hand on her shoulder. "Me too. Mmm …
tacos. Want us to set the table, Nan?"

"Sure. Maybe Kate can get Pete. He's been in his room playing since we got home. Ask him to wash up and come eat."

Kate took the stairs two at a time but slowed as she neared
Pete's door. No need to startle him. She turned the knob and
stepped into his neat room. No toys on the floor, the bed made.
It always amazed her how much her little brother loved order.
He couldn't stand having anything out of place. No Pete in sight.
Must be in the bathroom.

She headed down the hall and paused outside the closed
door, rapping on it twice. "Hey, Pete, lunch is ready. It's your
favorite, tacos."

No response.

Kate waited, counting to ten, then tapped again. "Come on,
Pete. We're hungry."

Still no answer.

This had happened before. Pete had locked himself in the
bathroom and wouldn't reply or come out. She stepped to the
top of the landing and leaned over. "Mom? Pete's in the bathroom and won't answer me."

Footfalls sounded on the bottom step, and Dad appeared in
the stairwell. "I'll get him. You go down and help your mother
finish up."

Kate passed him in the hall and bolted down the stairs, her stomach reminding her that it had been hours since breakfast.

Two minutes passed without her dad or Pete coming down. Kate looked at her mom. "What's up with Pete? It's not like him to not want to come eat lunch."

Mom shrugged. "I'm not sure. He's always quiet, but the last couple of days, it seems like he's been more bothered than normal."

Feet thudded on the floor above them. "Nan! Pete's not here!"

Chapter Nine

Kate stared at her mother, who'd stopped pouring the home-canned salsa into a bowl. "What's going on? Where's Pete?"

Her dad entered the room and echoed the question.

"Did you check our bedroom?" Mom's lips pinched together. "He may have gone to get the book we were reading together and fallen asleep on our bed."

Dad pivoted and headed toward the hall. "You're probably right."

Kate leaned her elbow on the countertop. "I hope they hurry. I'm starved."

Dad appeared in the doorway again, his brows drawn in worry. "He's not there, Nan. And I checked the downstairs bathroom too. Do you think he went to the backyard or the barn?"

Mom looked out the window. "It's possible, but he would have taken Rufus, and the dog's asleep on the porch. I don't like this, John." She grabbed her jacket and opened the front door. "Pete? Where are you?"

Dad followed her, with Kate on his heels.

Kate's stomach twisted into a knot, all thought of food forgotten. She shoved her hands into the arms of the coat she'd removed only minutes earlier. Pete was probably hiding in the barn or yard, but something didn't feel right. He hadn't done anything like this in a couple of years. "Rufus, come on, boy. Let's go find Pete. Dad, I'm going to check the barn. He might be playing in there."

"Good idea. His coat wasn't on the hook, so if he's outside, at least he won't be cold."

Kate jogged across the open area between the house and the barn, and Rufus loped along beside her. The people door to the side of the big main doors that led into the arena stood open. Her shoulders slumped in relief. Her little brother had to be inside.

She stepped into the dim interior and allowed her eyes to adjust. "Pete? Are you in here, buddy? Tell Kate where you are, okay?" More than likely he wouldn't reply, but she kept calling just the same. "Pete! Quit hiding now and come out. Mom made tacos for lunch."

She poked her head into the first stall, with no results. As she continued on down the aisle running in front of the stalls and checked each one, worry set in again, big-time. No brown-haired brother looked up from whatever might have drawn him here. "Rufus, find Pete. Where's Pete, Rufus?"

The dog nosed around and whined, then gazed up at her, tail wagging. Kate closed the final stall door and headed to the steps leading into the loft where hay used to be kept. Maybe Pete had fallen asleep in some of the old straw still scattered on the floor upstairs. She thought for sure Mom and Dad would have hollered by now, letting her know they'd found him.

The big outside door into the arena rolled open a little, and Dad poked his head in. "You find him yet?" Worry clouded his words. "He's not in the yard anywhere, and we went through the house again. Nothing."

Kate bolted up the wood stairs toward the loft. "No. I've checked all the stalls and the tack room. It will only take me a couple minutes to search the loft." She heard Dad thudding up the steps behind her, but she kept going, hitting the top one and launching herself across the floor, fear hot on her heels. Where was her brother hiding? They'd searched everywhere, with no sign of him.

"He's not here, Dad."

"Are you sure?" Dad strode across the straw-littered floor and headed toward a dark corner. "Pete? Answer me, Son." He stooped and peered into the dim corner. "You're right."

"Where is he, Dad? What's happened to Pete?" Her voice choked on the last word, and her heart pounded, ready to explode.

Kate, her mother, and her father stood outside the barn door. Her normally calm mom was shaking, and her face was white. Dad didn't look much better, and Kate felt like she might hurl. Pete had never left their yard alone and rarely even went outside without one of his family members or Rufus along. "What do we do next, Dad?"

"I think I'd better call the sheriff."

Mom nodded. "Good idea. It won't be dark for hours, but he's only six. I'm so—" She glanced at Kate and stopped.

Kate stared at her. "It's okay, Mom. I'm scared too. This is awful. I'm going to call Tori and ask her to keep an eye out. Pete walked over there with me once, and he might have decided to go visit on his own."

Mom blinked a couple of times as though trying to gather her thoughts. "That can't hurt. I'll call the pastor and ask if he can get some of the people from church to start searching or to keep an eye out. I'll use my cell, Dad can use his, and you use the landline, Kate."

Kate hurried into the living room and snatched the phone with trembling hands. "Oh, God, please take care of Pete." She whispered the words, almost afraid to admit out loud that anything could happen to her sweet little brother. Sure, like any brother, he was annoying at times, but she loved him a lot. No way did she want him hurt or lost or scared. If someone found him, he wouldn't even be able to give them his address or explain where he lived. She punched in Tori's number and waited. One ring. Two. Three. Four. *Hurry up and answer!*

"Hello?"

"Tori, I'm so glad I got you. Pete's missing. He took off by himself while Mom was fixing lunch. She thought he was upstairs playing in his room, but he's gone. Can you please keep watch around your house and let us know if he comes by?"

Tori gasped. "Hold on." Her muffled voice sounded in the background for a minute. Then she came back on the line. "Mom's here. She's going to start walking toward your house, and I'm coming with her. We'll have Mom's cell phone. You have the number, right?"

"Right."

Kate's mother stepped into the room. "Has Tori seen any sign of him, Kate?"

"Hold on, Tori." She repeated what Tori had said to her mother.

"Tell her we'll walk toward their house. We can cover the distance between us much faster that way. I'll have my cell, and anyone who spots Pete should call the other. Got that?"

Kate dipped her head and passed the information to her friend, then hung up. "They're getting coats and heading out right now. How about Dad?"

He appeared in the doorway beside Kate's mom. "I'll wait here for the sheriff. He and I are going to cruise the neighborhood. You guys take off, and call me if you find anything."

Kate and her mother raced across the front porch and down the path. Then her mom inhaled and slowed. Kate grabbed her hand. "Hey, let's hurry up."

"We need to take it slow. He could be hiding anywhere or have fallen and hurt himself. If we run, we could miss him."

As much as Kate wanted to argue, she understood. She hated the thought of moving like a slug when all she wanted to do was run, call Pete's name, and find him, but she did as her mother suggested. "Okay, fine. But let's holler for him. Maybe he'll hear us and come out of hiding if he's along the road and scared."

Mom nodded. "You stay here. I'm going to cover the other side of the road. Be sure you check the ditches and behind any big clumps of brush."

"Shouldn't we check with the neighbors up the road?"

"Dad's taking care of that. He said the sheriff is sending a deputy to each house close by to ask if they've seen Pete."

"Good." Kate left the edge of the road and circled a clump of five fir trees. "Pete? Come out if you're hiding. It's time to go home."

They'd covered half the distance before they spotted Tori and her mother coming toward them, each on opposite sides of the road. Kate bounded forward and halted beside her friend. "Did you see anything?"

"Not a thing. Sorry, Kate. Has Pete run away before? Where do you think he'd go?"

Kate's mother and Mrs. Velasquez joined them in time to hear Tori's question. Kate looked at her mother. "He's never run away, and I have no idea where he might go. Do you, Mom?"

"I've been thinking about that ever since we left the house. If he didn't go to Tori's house, there's only one other place he's walked to, since we always drive to church."

Kate stared at her mother for a long moment, then blurted what she knew her mother was thinking. "My horse." She motioned to Tori. "I took Pete for a walk one day, and we took carrots to the mare we found in the paddock. I told him I wished she could be my horse someday."

Mom's face set in firm lines. "I didn't know you told him that, Kate, but it makes sense. He's been talking a lot about

Kate's horse lately. I thought at first he meant the horse cake you had for your birthday, and then that he was thinking about the job you turned down at the barn." She glanced at Tori's mother. "That the girls turned down." She turned her attention back to Kate. "Now I think he might have been talking about the mare. Let's get over there as fast as we can, and I'll call your dad and let him know where we're headed."

Kate's heart thudded. She could barely breathe. Was it her fault her little brother ran away and put himself in danger? She hadn't told her mother the complete truth. She never should have taken him to see that mare.

Chapter Ten

The girls moved from a fast walk to a jog, with their mothers following close behind, as they closed the distance to the pen containing the mare. What if Pete wasn't there? Would Mom fall apart, and would Dad yell at Kate? He'd never really yelled in his life that Kate could remember, but Pete had never gone missing like this either.

Tori nudged her in the side. "Are you praying? God's going to help us find your brother, you know."

Kate stared at her new friend, both grateful and ashamed that Tori had to remind her. "I feel awful. I haven't really prayed since we started. I keep thinking it's my fault. I wanted a horse so bad, and I told him I wished the mare would belong to me someday. I'm not sure Pete understood she isn't mine. He's been worried about her since I brought him over. He loves animals, even if he doesn't talk much."

Tori nodded. "Yeah, I know what you mean. Pete seems like a good kid. There's more than one person at school with an autistic brother or sister."

"I know," Kate said. Her mom tapped her on her shoulder, and she glanced back. "We're almost there, Mom. Right around this next corner."

"Let's hurry up. We don't have time to visit." Mom's normally happy tone was edged with fear.

Kate bit her lip. "Sure. Come on, Tori. Let's run the rest of the way."

The girls increased their pace to a steady, smooth run, and Kate was surprised to see both her mother and Mrs. Velasquez keeping pace behind them. "Wow, your mom can move."

Tori grinned. "She used to play softball and still runs every morning."

They rounded the final corner, and Kate's heart dropped to her toes. The mare stood next to the fence, but there was no sign of Pete—not from what she could see.

They were still at least a hundred feet away when Mom gasped and raced past Kate. "Pete. Peter! Baby, are you okay?"

A dark-green mound on the ground near the post moved, and Pete sat up. It looked like he'd curled into a ball under the lowest rail. Kate arrived a few seconds after her mother, in time to see her scoop Pete into her arms and hug him. It didn't seem to matter to her that Pete didn't reply.

Kate patted his back. "You okay, bud? You're not hurt, are you?"

Pete shook his head. "Your horse is hungry." He squirmed in his mother's arms until she set him down. He dug into his pocket and withdrew a carrot. "Pete brought food."

Kate knelt in front of him, not caring that the moisture on the grass seeped through her jeans. "Why did you come without me? You could have gotten hurt all by yourself."

"Kate is sad she can't work at the barn."

"But I still would have brought you over here if you'd asked me to." She touched his cheek, but he pulled away.

"No. I gonna bring Kate her horse." He took a long piece of twine from his pocket.

Mrs. Velasquez edged closer. "That horse is too big for you, Pete. It might have stepped on you if you let it out of the pen."

Pete twisted his hands together. "Kate teach me."

Mom glared at Kate. "Did you let him lead that horse?"

"No! I showed him how to hold his hand flat and feed her a carrot, that's all. I'd never do anything that would put him in danger." She tried to look in Pete's eyes, but he turned his head away. "The horse is too big for you to bring home, bud. But thank you for caring."

"Kate work at the barn and learn. Pete learn too."

Kate glanced at Tori's mom and her mother, not sure what to say. This was the most her brother had ever said at one time. She was thrilled but also a little bummed that she couldn't assure him that what he'd said would happen.

"We'll talk about it later, okay, Pete?" Mom took his hand, and he didn't resist. "Are you ready to go home now and have some lunch?"

He dropped his head, and his favorite tuneless half-dozen notes came through his tightly pressed lips. Her little brother had gone back into his own safe world, and who knew how long it would be before he'd come out again.

Mrs. Velasquez touched Tori's shoulder. "Honey, would you and Kate mind taking Pete and going ahead of us so I can talk to Mrs. Ferris?" She swiveled toward Kate's mom. "If you don't mind, that is?"

Mom hesitated, then nodded. "That's fine, as long as they stay close where I can keep an eye on him. I don't want you to get more than a couple of steps ahead, okay, girls?" She withdrew her cell phone from her pocket. "Before we go anywhere, I'll call Dad and let him know we found Pete. It's not far to the house, so I'll have him meet us there."

"Sure, Mom." Kate took Pete's hand. He didn't respond in any way as her hand gently took his, but he didn't pull away, and

Kate released a happy sigh. Kate sure was glad Mom insisted they stay close and not get too far ahead. She secretly hoped to hear what Tori's mom wanted to discuss.

When her mother got off the phone, they struck off up the road, and the gravel crunched under the two women's feet behind the girls and Pete. Tori shot Kate a warning with her lips extended in a *shhh* motion, and Kate gave an ever-so-slight nod. It was obvious Tori wanted to listen too, and Kate was more than good with that. With the mood Pete was in, he wasn't going to say a thing to break the stillness.

Mrs. Velasquez cleared her throat. "I am so sorry for all the worry you've gone through today on account of your little boy. But I don't understand why he came here. This isn't your daughter's horse, is it? Have you agreed to purchase the horse from the owner?"

"No. We're not even sure who owns it. My husband has been asking around."

Kate held her breath, praying her mother would say Dad planned to buy the mare when he found out.

"Kate's been so worried because the mare is thin, and she's right. Whoever owns it isn't taking proper care of her, although I was happy to see the mare had been fed and the water tank was full."

Kate stopped and whirled, pulling Pete with her. "I didn't see any hay. How do you know that, Mom?"

Mom leveled a stern gaze at her. "You shouldn't be interrupting, but considering it's so important to you, I'll let it go this time. You were focused on Pete, but while you were talking to him, I noticed a lot of fine pieces of hay littering the ground inside the lean-to. It looks like the mare's been fed lately, so someone must be caring for her now."

"But she's still too thin, and her hooves are in terrible shape, like they haven't been trimmed for months. They're long and starting to break, and her coat and mane are rough."

"Yes, I noticed all of that, but at least we can be grateful she's being fed."

"Yeah, but for how long? Mom, what guarantee is there she'll get fed tomorrow or the next day?" Kate pleaded. "I'm going to come by here after school every day next week and check on her."

"I don't have a problem with that, but you and Tori and Pete need to get moving, or Dad is going to worry."

"Okay." The girls started walking again, but Kate kept an ear tuned behind her.

They covered some yards in silence before Mrs. Velasquez spoke again. "How did you learn so much about horses? Aren't you afraid? I would have been screaming if my little boy had been lying so close to that horse's feet."

"Thankfully he wasn't under the rail and inside her pen, or I might have been. You can never completely trust any horse, but learning ways to be safe and how to handle one takes much of the risk away."

"You mean like the girls working at the barn?"

Kate held her breath, even more afraid to miss Mom's answer this time around.

"Yes, exactly. That's a very controlled environment. They'd be cleaning stalls and grooming horses that are tied up, all under supervision. You asked how I know so much. I was raised around horses. My dad had a small stable. Nothing like the one where Kate and Tori want to work, but we had several head that he boarded. We didn't have a trainer or anything fancy, but I rode for years before I went away to college."

"Why did you quit? Or do you still ride?"

"I enjoyed riding, but it wasn't important to me like it is to Kate. It's her dream and passion. Mine was to get married, raise a family, and be a good mom."

Pete dragged his feet against the gravel, kicking rocks and shuffling. Kate glanced at Tori, who peeked sideways at her, then Tori looked back at her mother.

"Tori told me that Kate refused to take the job at the barn if Tori couldn't do it too." Tori's mom sounded somber and a little sad.

"Yes, Kate told me she made that promise."

"I don't want to see your girl not be able to follow her dream because of my fear."

"Do you mind if I ask why you're afraid?" Mom's words were dipped in kindness.

"It's hard to talk about, but yes, I'll tell you. My little brother fell off a horse when he was young. He was in the hospital for a long time with a head injury, and I was sure he'd die."

"But he lived?" Mom asked.

"Yes. He was riding in an open field, and he kicked the horse in the sides to make him run. The horse tripped in a gopher hole. Miguel flew over his head and struck a rock. You see why I don't want Victoria to ride?"

Mom was quiet for a minute before she replied. "I can understand why you'd be afraid, but there's something you haven't thought of." She drew in a long, slow breath. "I imagine if your brother had taken lessons, he wouldn't have forced his horse to run across an open field that he wasn't familiar with, especially if he wasn't a good rider. The instructor might have kept him in an enclosed area while he learned to ride, the way Tori would be if she worked at the barn. Tori and Kate will also be required to wear helmets when they ride, to protect their heads from injury."

Tori's mom murmured something that Kate didn't hear. She wanted to whirl around and beg Mrs. Velasquez to reconsider, but she knew what her mother would say. It wasn't her place to interrupt again. Instead, maybe this would be a good time to pray as Tori had suggested.

Chapter Eleven

Kate's dad met them a block from their house and knelt in front of Pete, gently gripping his upper arms. "Are you okay, little guy?"

Pete nodded but kept his face averted. "Want to save Kate's horse. She's hungry. Pete's hungry too." He tugged away from his father and marched toward the house, but Mom grasped his wrist. "Not so fast, Peter. We'll all stay together, all right? No more going off by yourself."

Dad grinned at Mom. "I guess he's fine, huh?"

Mom nodded. "I've never been so grateful for anything in my life. He gave us all a scare." She turned to Mrs. Velasquez and Tori, who'd stopped close together. "Thank you both for coming and helping us search. You're wonderful neighbors, and I hope"—she directed her words toward Tori's mom—"that we'll become friends."

The other woman nodded and smiled. "*Si*. I feel the same way. You must come visit sometime. My home is humble, but you will be welcome." She placed her arm across Tori's shoulders. "I will think on what you have said and talk to my husband again. May I call you later tonight?"

Dad eyed Mom, but she simply said, "Thank you. That would be nice."

Kate could barely keep quiet. She wanted to grab Tori, drag her to the side, and ask what she thought. Had Mom changed Mrs. Velasquez's mind about Tori working at the barn, or was she only going to call to invite her mother to tea or something just as boring?

Tori met her eyes and barely hunched one shoulder.

Kate mouthed two words, praying her friend could read lips. *Call me.*

Tori raised her hand. "Later." She touched Pete on the top of his head. "'Bye, Pete. No more hunting for horses, okay? If you want to go over there again, you ask me or Kate, and we'll take you if your mom or dad says so."

Pete kept his chin tucked against his chest and rocked from his toes to his heels and back again, humming his favorite melody.

A couple of hours later, the phone rang, and Mom picked it up before Kate had a chance to grab it. She listened for a moment, then handed the receiver to Kate. "It's Tori."

"I'll take it to my room."

Her mother nodded, and Kate raced across the living room.

"Hey, Tori, what's going on with your mom?" Kate blurted out even before she got her door closed.

"Well, hi to you too." Tori broke into laughter on her end of the line.

"Come on, spill! I've been dying since I got home." Kate flopped against her pillows.

"She changed her mind. She said yesss!" Tori yelled out the last word.

Kate held the phone away from her ear and grinned. Slowly she returned it and listened to make sure Tori wouldn't scream again, although she wanted to let out some whoops herself. "No way! Seriously? Oh man, I can't believe it!" Kate sat up and then threw herself against the pillows again. "Wow! Did she say why?"

"Yeah. We had a long talk after she talked to my dad. He told her he didn't see any reason why I shouldn't work at the barn. When Mom saw how upset Pete was and listened to what your mom had to say, she couldn't say no. I am beyond excited!"

"That makes two of us. It's probably too late tonight, but I'll call Mrs. Wilder in the morning before we go to school. Just think … we'll be starting at the barn in two days." There was a long silence, and Kate wondered if Tori had hung up. "Hey? You still there? What's up?"

"Yeah, I'm here." Tori paused, then, "Do you think she's still going to let us work if we don't call until tomorrow?"

Kate could barely contain her excitement. "Dad told her he'd appreciate another day or so, and she said it was okay, so I think we're good."

"Whew. I'd better go. Mom's giving me 'the look,' but I'll sleep a lot better tonight knowing we get to do this. And that your brother's safe too, of course."

Kate sobered. "I know. And tell your parents thanks for me, will you?" She disconnected and headed back to the living room to hang up the phone. At last things were going their way. Now if she could find a way to rescue that mare, life would be perfect. Even if Mom thought someone was feeding the horse, she was still too thin and obviously neglected. It wasn't right leaving her cooped up in a small pen with only a rickety lean-to for shelter and feeding her whenever someone happened to remember. Not right at all.

And Kate intended to do something to change that.

Chapter Twelve

When Kate and Tori stepped into the barn on Tuesday afternoon, they met Mrs. Wilder, her face beaming. "I'm so glad you made it, girls. I was hoping nothing would happen to change your decision between yesterday morning and this afternoon. I hired another person to help clean stalls and groom as well, and I'll introduce you in a bit."

Kate peeked at Tori, wondering what she thought of this new turn of events, but her friend didn't reply. She hadn't heard any of the girls at school talking about working at the barn. It might be nice to meet another girl their age who loved horses as much as she did. Of course, it could be an older person too.

Kate smiled at Mrs. Wilder. "We can't wait to get started."

Tori nodded. "I'm sorry it took us so long to make a decision. My mom wasn't sure at first how she felt about me working around horses."

Mrs. Wilder cocked her head. "And she's all right with it now?"

"Yes. She talked to Kate's mom and understands that everything we do here will be supervised. At first she thought we'd be handling a lot of horses on our own and might get hurt. She's cool with it now, though."

"Today you'll only be cleaning stalls. I'll be sending a parental release form home with you when you're done, and you won't be allowed around any of the horses until that's signed. I should have sent it with you on Saturday, and I apologize for forgetting." She started up the aisle and beckoned for the girls to follow. "I'll show you where to start and introduce you to our other worker."

Kate glanced at Tori and leaned close to whisper, "She didn't say anything about a release form when we were here last time."

Tori lifted a shoulder. "Maybe they're worried about getting sued."

"Yeah, no doubt."

Horses stomped and nickered from the stalls as they walked past, and Kate slowed to check each one, her heart rate accelerating. This was a dream come true. She could hardly believe she was actually here, ready to start working toward taking lessons and maybe one day having her own horse.

Mrs. Wilder paused at the door to the tack room. "There's something I forgot to mention on Saturday." She stepped inside and waited for the girls to enter. "We installed security cameras in here a few weeks ago. Someone broke into the barn one night in February and stole two show saddles and matching bridle sets. Our tack is insured, but we don't want it to happen again." The woman waved them back out into the aisle. "We ask all of the people who help out to keep a watchful eye open for strangers who appear to be snooping around. If someone looks suspicious, come directly to me and report it. Understood?"

Both girls nodded. They followed her to the end of the barn and stopped in front of the large, open room that contained a mound of wood shavings that reached halfway up the walls. Two wheelbarrows and three shovels were positioned inside the door.

A cheery whistle trilled outside the open doorway, and seconds later a slender, redheaded boy about their age swung into sight. He lifted a hand and grinned, the freckles on his cheeks dancing. "Hi, Mrs. Wilder. I hope I'm not late."

Tori stared at the boy, but Kate saw no sign of recognition light her friend's eyes.

Mrs. Wilder shook her head. "You're right on time, Colt. These two young ladies were anxious to start and arrived ahead of schedule. Now that you're here, we'll get started." She turned to the girls. "Do you already know Colt Turner?"

"No." Both girls spoke at the same time.

The boy's grin widened. "We've only lived in Odell for a few months, and my mom homeschools me and my little sister, so I haven't gotten acquainted with very many kids my age yet."

Kate smiled. "I'm Kate Ferris, and this is my friend Tori Velasquez. I moved here in March, but Tori's lived in Odell her whole life."

Mrs. Wilder gestured toward the wheelbarrows. "Fill those up. Girls, you'll take charge of one, and Colt can take the other. He'll work on one stall by himself, and you girls will do the next one after. You'll go down the full row of stalls this afternoon. Another employee will turn the horses out in the indoor arena before you start cleaning and put them back in their stalls when you're done. You'll go in and strip everything out of the stalls first and dump the contents outside this door in the pile you'll see. When the stall is stripped to the rubber mats, then bring four full wheelbarrows of clean shavings in and spread them across the floor. Got that?"

The three nodded. Colt placed a widemouthed shovel in the wheelbarrow and then grabbed the handles. "Ready when you are."

Kate grabbed two shovels while Tori pushed the wheelbarrow behind Colt as he headed toward the first stall. She and Tori wheeled on past him to the open door of the second stall, then Tori paused. "Gross. I should have worn rubber boots, not my old sneakers. And it stinks." She pointed at a large damp spot that covered one entire corner that was also littered with manure.

Kate shrugged. "Thankfully we won't have to step in any of it—only slide the shovel in and clean it out from the door to the corners."

The boy next door chuckled. "You'll get used to it. Soon you won't even notice the smell. I wear my old cowboy boots, but you're right about not stepping in any of it."

Kate backed into the alleyway and peered into his stall. "You're wearing cowboy boots? Do you ride? You sound like you've been around barns before."

Colt kept shoveling, tossing each full scoop into his wheelbarrow. "Yes to both, and I ride Western. But if you don't hurry up, I'll be done before the two of you are." He gave a wicked smile. "Boys are naturally better workers."

Kate planted her hands on her hips and glared until she saw him struggling to keep his smile from erupting. "Right. We'll show you who is best, won't we, Tori?" She spun and bolted into the stall.

"No kidding!" Tori scooped the first full shovel of dirty shavings from their stall and plopped them into the wheelbarrow. "We'll be done first."

Colt's laugh echoed through the walls. "You'd better be started on the next one by the time I finish this if you expect to win."

The girls went to work with determination, digging into the mess on the floor and filling the wheelbarrow, but Colt was pushing his toward the outdoor refuse pile seconds before they headed that direction.

Kate rolled her eyes at Tori. "We're going to have to hurry it up."

Tori headed down the aisle at a trot, with Kate close beside. All of a sudden, the top-heavy wheelbarrow started to tip sideways. Tori let out a shriek. "It's going to spill!"

Kate tried to grab the edge, but it was too late. Shavings and manure tumbled over the side as the entire contraption hit the floor. Kate jumped back, but not before some of the material scattered over her hands and arms and cascaded down her jeans. "Eww! Totally gross!"

Chapter Thirteen

Kate stared at the mess scattered across the full width of the aisle running between the stalls and the indoor arena and groaned. "Mrs. Wilder will fire us if she sees this." She hoisted the wheelbarrow back into an upright position.

Tori grabbed the shovel and started scooping. "I guess we got it too heavy, and it overbalanced. I'm so sorry, Kate!"

"It would've happened to either of us, so don't sweat it. I've never pushed anything that full either." She ran back to the stall and returned with the second shovel. The two girls scrambled to clean the area, praying Mrs. Wilder wouldn't show up before they finished.

Footsteps farther along the alleyway made Kate freeze, and she slowly swiveled, then drooped with relief. "Oh, it's you."

Colt pushed his wheelbarrow toward them. "Uh, *yeah*. You were expecting someone else?" He stopped and thumped the legs of his wheelbarrow down next to theirs, then withdrew his shovel and went to work.

Tori paused, her mouth hanging open. "Hey, we made the mess, not you. You won the race to get the stall cleaned, and you don't have to help."

He shrugged. "Maybe I want to."

Kate stared. "Well, okay then. Thanks." She pushed her shovel under another mound and scooped it up. "You want to work together after this?"

His face brightened. "Sure. It'd be more fun that way, if you don't mind."

They collected the last of the pile and wheeled toward the exit. Kate motioned toward Colt. "You didn't bring any shavings back."

"Naw. I didn't heap mine as full as yours, so I still have more to clean."

Kate huffed. "Guess that's smart."

The next minutes passed in silence as the trio finished cleaning one stall and then the other. After they'd returned with full loads of shavings and spread them, Kate surveyed the clean area. "Sure wish we could lead the horses in and out and do more than clean stalls."

Tori shuddered. "I don't. At least not yet. Look at that thing!" She pointed at the far end of the arena where a tall

Thoroughbred raced in a circle, bucking and kicking. "My mom was right. Those things can kill you."

Colt edged up beside her. "He's glad to be out of his stall, is all. Once he has a halter on, he's probably fine. Besides, that mare out there is practically asleep. He can't be too dangerous, or she'd be staying clear of him."

Kate studied Colt for the first time since they'd been introduced. She guessed he might be about thirteen. He was dressed in dusty jeans, a T-shirt, and worn cowboy boots, and wore his hair short. Good thing, as it looked like he'd probably have some serious curls going on if he let it grow out. He wasn't what other girls might consider to be hot, but his blue eyes sparkled, and his grin was pretty cute. And he didn't act a bit stuck-up or rude like some boys she'd met. "You act like you know a lot about horses."

"I've got one back home."

"Isn't this home?" Tori kicked at a pile of clean shavings, smoothing it out.

He tossed the shovels over his shoulder. "I suppose it is now. We'd better get to the next stall. Looks like they're catching the two horses that belong in here."

The girls hurried after him and waited for him to slide the next stall door open before they entered and got busy.

Once they were shoveling again, Kate asked Colt, "Where's home?"

"Montana." His lips twisted to the side. "Only it's here now. My dad took a job as an accountant with a company in Hood River, so we moved. My horse is still back home at a friend's. My parents said we can have him trailered out this summer, but we've got to find a place to keep him."

Kate dumped a scoop of dirty shavings into the wheelbarrow. "How about here?"

"I talked to Mrs. Wilder about it, but it's too expensive. I was hoping to work off some of his board, but I can't put in enough hours to do that and pay for his feed and everything else. I'm not sure what we're going to do."

Tori huffed as she lifted an overly full shovel. "This stuff is heavy when it's wet."

"Yeah." Kate placed the last shovelful on top of the growing pile. "We'd better stop now, or we'll have another accident." She peered out into the alleyway. "That gorgeous horse is coming in, so don't go out there yet."

A young woman wearing riding breeches and a jacket led the gray Thoroughbred toward them. It snorted and pranced for a couple of steps, then settled and followed the girl to his stall.

Tori moved toward the handler. "What's his name?"

"Rocket." The girl slid the door shut and hung the halter on a horseshoe hook on the outside. "That's his nickname, not his registered name. He was a racehorse that didn't live up to his name, but we saved him from slaughter and turned him into a great jumper." She eyed Kate, Tori, and Colt. "You the new kids who'll be cleaning stalls?"

Tori nodded. "Yeah. On Tuesdays and Thursdays after school and Saturday mornings."

The girl nodded. "I'm Carissa Spencer. I exercise the horses when their owners aren't here to ride them."

Kate dusted her hands against her jeans, suddenly aware of how dirty they all appeared next to this attractive girl who must have been out of high school. "Are you a trainer?"

"No, although I hope to be someday, if I can ever afford a horse like Rocket. The trainer is here most mornings, and there's usually a groom around then. It's pretty quiet this time of day, but it'll get busy again in the evening when people are off work and come to use the arena." She waved and headed back toward the arena. "I'll bring in Athena and then take the next two horses out so you can keep cleaning."

Kate waved toward the empty stall they'd been working on. "Where's the one that belongs here?"

"He's in an outdoor paddock. We turn Athena and Rocket out together because they're buddies, but most of the horses have to be turned out alone. We don't need any kicking matches where a boarder's horse gets a leg broken. You guys be careful around the horses until you know which ones are safe to handle and which ones to stay away from."

Tori shuddered and her face paled. "I think I'm gonna be sick. Maybe I made the wrong decision coming to work here, Kate. Can we please finish cleaning and go home?"

Chapter Fourteen

Kate had barely slept for the past two nights, and she'd dragged all through the morning classes at school, worried that Tori would stick to her decision to quit working at the barn. If that happened, she supposed she could team up with Colt, but she wanted Tori to continue. It wouldn't be the same without her new best friend. Most girls her age cared more about boys or makeup or new clothes than horses, but Kate had never wanted anything as much as she wanted these riding lessons. Tori had swung from quitting to working to quitting again but had promised she'd give Kate a final answer at lunch break today.

Kate waited in the lunchroom and peered toward the entrance, not wanting to miss Tori. Her stomach was tied in knots, and if she tried to eat right now, she'd hurl. A group of girls, whispering and giggling, entered the room, but no sign of Tori.

Someone tugged on her hair, and Kate whirled. "Tori! How'd you get in here without me seeing you?"

Tori smirked. "Guess you must have missed me among all the dark-haired girls wandering around." She sobered and tugged at Kate's arm. "Come on, I'm starving."

Kate shook her head. "No way. I can't eat until you give me your answer."

Tori's arm fell to her side. "Yeah. Sorry. Guess I should have done that first."

Kate's heart sank at her friend's serious tone. "I think I can guess."

"Think so, huh?" Tori flashed a smile. "Gotcha! I'm sticking it out, Kate. I'm not going to be a quitter. Besides, I don't want my mom to say, 'I told you so.'"

Kate would have hugged Tori if there weren't so many people around. "You totally had me scared. Let's grab some food before we both starve. I can't wait for school to be over so we can head to the barn."

Thursday's time spent at the barn hadn't brought any more problems, and Saturday had dawned bright and clear. Kate could hardly wait for their two hours of work to be finished so she and Tori could take their first lesson. She hadn't thought to ask Colt if he was taking lessons, but since he had his own horse, it didn't seem likely. It had been nice working with Tori and getting to know Colt while cleaning stalls. He seemed like a good guy.

Tori lightly punched her arm. "Earth to Kate. Wake up. We're not finished cleaning this stall yet. What are you thinking about, anyway? You have a silly smile on your face."

Kate hated to admit she'd been thinking it was nice to have another friend besides Tori, even if he was a boy. Not that boys weren't okay, but she'd never been interested in having a boy-friend. Not yet. Colt was someone fun to hang around with at work because he had a good sense of humor and teased her, kind of like her dad. The last thing she wanted Tori to think was that she was interested in Colt as more than a friend. "I'm glad we get to take our first lesson today. I can't wait."

Colt pushed his full wheelbarrow to the opening of their stall and set it down. "I'm taking lessons too. I wonder if we'll all be doing it at the same time."

Tori shook her head. "Kate and I are both riding Lulu, so unless Mrs. Wilder has us riding double, I doubt it."

Colt motioned down the aisle. "The POA down at the end?"

Kate nodded. "Yeah. How about you?"

"I'm not sure, but since I'm taller than either of you, I'm guessing my feet would be close to dragging the ground if I rode her."

Kate tossed the final shovelful of manure into the wheelbarrow, thankful this was their last stall. "What kind of horse do you own?"

"A Quarter horse gelding named Romeo." He scowled. "And no, I didn't name him. I wanted to change it, but the person who owned him went on and on about how he knows his name and would be confused, so I kept it. He *is* pretty smart, and he acts like he knows it, so I guess it was the right decision. But it's still pretty weird."

Kate and Tori looked at each other and then broke out in a laugh. Kate covered her mouth with her hand. "Sorry. I'm not making fun. It's just …" She snorted another laugh through her fingers.

"I know, I know." He jerked his chin toward the big outside door. "Come on. Let's go dump this stuff and get the shavings."

Tori grabbed the handles of the wheelbarrow. "Right."

They got done in record time, then headed toward Lulu's stall. They'd cleaned it first thing this morning, but Mrs. Wilder had told them to come back when they finished to groom the mare and clean her feet. She'd already checked Colt out on handling Lulu and had instructed him to show the girls what to do.

Kate slipped the halter over the pony's head and buckled it, then led her into the alleyway.

Colt grabbed a cross tie from a post next to the arena and motioned Tori toward the outer stall wall. "Clip that cross tie on the side ring of her halter, and I'll do the same on this side. That way she can't move forward or backward more than a step."

"I'll grab the tack box." Kate headed to the tack room next to Lulu's stall, remembering what Mrs. Wilder had said about the security cameras. It felt strange knowing someone might be watching her every move to see if she touched something she shouldn't. She walked straight to the row of shelves against the back wall and lifted the open carry case full of grooming tools, then hurried back to Tori and Colt. "I think this has all the brushes and hoof picks we need." She set the case on the floor off to the side of Lulu's front feet. "I groomed a horse a few times in Spokane, but I'm not sure which brushes to use."

Colt picked up a flat, black rubber thing shaped like an oval with short teeth on one side. "This is a currycomb. If the horse has dried mud or sweat, you'd want to use this, or if it's shedding and you're trying to loosen the dead hair." He placed the curry on Lulu's neck and started stroking, using light pressure. "When you get to her body, you can go in circles and push a little harder. Don't ever use this on her face or her legs. You only want to use soft brushes there." They watched as he finished running the curry all over Lulu. "See? She isn't shedding much yet. Kate, get a stiff brush from the box, and Tori, would you get a soft one?"

They both did as asked and waited. Colt stepped to the side and nodded at Kate. "Take the stiff brush and run it down her neck, then over her withers and back, and under her belly and over her hip. Then Tori will do the same thing with the soft brush to finish her off."

Tori wrinkled her nose. "I have no idea where her withers are, and I don't see why she needs so much brushing. I don't even brush my hair this much!"

"Brushing not only gets rid of loose hair; it brings the oil in their skin to the surface, which keeps their coat in good condition. Mrs. Wilder said they turn the horses out in the fields and paddocks when the weather is dry. I guess they rotate them between the daytime and night, so all the horses have a chance to get outside. So if she comes in muddy or sweaty, you'd use the curry first."

"That makes sense. But I still don't know what her withers are," Tori said.

Kate ran the brush over the bump at the base of Lulu's neck. "Right here. It's this bone that's higher than her back or neck, see?"

Colt nodded. "That's where you measure her to see how tall she is. You go from the ground to the top of the withers and divide by four inches. Every four inches is one hand."

"Mrs. Wilder said Lulu is thirteen hands, so that means she'd be"—Kate calculated in her head—"fifty-two inches tall. But she's a lot taller than that if you count her head."

Colt laughed and motioned to Tori to start with her soft brush. "Yeah, but that's not how you measure a horse. She looks pretty good. As soon as Tori finishes, we'll check her feet."

Tori swiped the last stroke down Lulu's hip. "Check them for what?"

"Mud or manure packed into their hooves." He plucked a curved tool with a point from the tack box. "This is a hoof pick." He stood next to Lulu's shoulder facing her rump and ran his hand down her front leg. As soon as he reached the joint above her hoof, she picked up her foot.

Tori laughed. "Wow! It looked like she picked it up by herself."

Colt grinned. "She did. All I did was squeeze. She's done it so often, she understands what I'm asking. If she didn't give easily, I'd put pressure on her shoulder, and that would make her do the same thing, because it shifts her weight off of that leg." He balanced her hoof on the palm of his hand and dug the pick into the packed material in the sole of her hoof. "See? Easy. One of you want to try?"

Tori held up her hands, palms out. "Not me. You go first, Kate, and I'll watch."

"Okay, but Mrs. Wilder said we both need to learn." Kate stepped alongside Lulu and imitated Colt's actions. "Hey, look! She picked her foot up!" Kate was so excited, she let go of the mare's leg, and her hoof thumped to the ground, barely missing Kate's toe. "Ugh. She almost stepped on me."

Colt nodded. "You've got to hold on to her leg. She won't hold it up by herself. And keep your toes back. You don't need to stand that close."

Kate tried again. "Cool! I've got it this time." She clutched the mare's leg and slid her hand under the hoof like Colt had shown her. "Give me the hoof pick." She took it from his outstretched hand. "There's nothing in there to get out. You already cleaned it."

"Yeah, but that doesn't matter. Just get the feel of it."

She did as he said and then gently let the mare's foot down until it rested on the floor. "That wasn't so hard. Your turn, Tori."

Tori shook her head. "I want to watch this time. I'm learning a lot, but I'm not ready to try it yet. I'll do it next time we come, okay?"

Colt shrugged. "I guess so. Here comes Mrs. Wilder, and she has someone with her."

Chapter Fifteen

Kate was in heaven. She was finally riding. An hour earlier Mrs. Wilder had introduced Mrs. Sorenson, the trainer. They'd gone through the steps of proper saddling and bridling, and now she was putting Kate and Lulu through their paces. Well, maybe not exactly Lulu's paces, because Lulu was finally off the lead line, and Kate was riding the mare around the arena by herself. Kate had been embarrassed when Mrs. Sorenson had snapped a long lunge line onto the side ring of the bridle to start the lesson.

Tori and Colt watched from the other side of the half wall separating the alleyway from the arena. Colt was smiling ear to ear, but Tori wore a troubled frown.

Kate saw her friend clearly as she rode past. "Tori, it's easy. Nothing to it. You're going to love it. Seriously!"

Tori shrugged but didn't reply.

Mrs. Sorenson was positioned in the center of one end of the arena as Kate continued around the half circle. "Have you trotted a horse before, Kate?"

"Yes. And I cantered once, but mostly I rode at a trot and a walk. I was starting to learn to post, but I'm not sure I understand that yet."

"Okay. Let's try a sitting trot. We'll want to work on your hands, your legs, your posture, and your seat before I ask you to post."

"Wow. That's a lot to think of at once." Tori spoke in a hesitant voice that carried across the intervening distance to Kate.

Mrs. Sorenson sent her a smile. "It is at first, but after a while, it's second nature. You won't even think about what you're doing. Pay attention to what I'm asking Kate to do, and it'll be easier when you take your lesson. Have you ridden before, Tori?"

Tori made a face. "Never."

The trainer nodded. "Are you excited to get started?"

"Uh ... not really. I never thought about riding a horse until I met Kate, but I'm willing to learn. It looks hard. I'm not sure I'll be any good at it."

Kate tried not to bounce as Lulu trotted around the circle. She wanted to say something to make Tori feel better, but she needed to concentrate on keeping her seat.

Colt had been quiet the entire time, but now he spoke. "Don't worry, Tori. When I first started riding, I thought the same thing, but it's not as hard as it seems."

Mrs. Sorenson signaled for Kate to halt. "Good job, Kate. You do a decent job sitting the trot. We need to work on teaching you to relax in the saddle and move with the horse, but that's a good start. Bring Lulu over to the gate so Tori can take her turn now."

Kate did as she was asked, all the time keeping her gaze on her friend. Tori looked like she was going to be sick, and Kate wondered if she'd done the right thing by pushing Tori to take this job. She'd seemed so excited at first, but then she got scared and almost quit, and now Tori was backing away toward the stalls instead of coming to meet her.

Colt's eyes met Kate's, then he glanced at Tori. He stepped toward her. "Hey, Tori." He dug into his pocket and hauled out a piece of carrot. "Give this to Lulu and make friends with her. She'll love you forever." He tossed her a saucy smirk.

Tori seemed to waver, but she quit backing up. "I'm not sure ..."

Kate halted the mare several paces from the rail, then dismounted, keeping a grip on the reins. "You don't have to do this if you don't want to, Tori. We can quit working here and bag this whole thing." Her body was trembling, but she wouldn't take back what she'd said. She'd had no idea Tori was so scared of riding.

Mrs. Sorenson moved up beside her and took Lulu's reins. "Tori? Are you ready?"

Tori blew out a long breath. "I'm no quitter. I'll do it if it kills me." She winced and then managed a feeble smile. "I mean, I hope it doesn't kill me." She stepped forward until she reached Lulu, then held the carrot on the palm of her hand under the horse's mouth. "Good girl, Lulu."

The mare took the treat without moving anything but her lips and munched it.

Tori sighed. "She doesn't seem too scary. I guess I can do this."

Kate grinned. "Sure you can. Lulu's a sweetheart." She retreated behind the half wall beside Colt.

Mrs. Sorenson helped Tori into the saddle and handed her the reins, then snapped the lunge line on again. "We'll take it nice and slow today and let you get used to being up there. If you want to, we'll only do a thirty-minute lesson today, and you can make up the rest another time."

"Yeah, that sounds good." Tori's pale face was a stark contrast to her dark hair. "Let's do this."

Thirty minutes later Kate could breathe easily again. She and Colt had kept completely silent during the lesson, and Kate had spent much of that time praying Tori would relax and enjoy riding Lulu. At least nothing terrible had happened, like falling off the pony. By the time Mrs. Sorenson showed her how to properly dismount, Tori appeared calmer.

Kate waited outside the ring, but as soon as Tori stopped beside her, she raised her hand. "High five! You did great!"

Tori slapped her hand in return. "Yeah. I'm still alive, and it wasn't as bad as I expected. In fact, once I was up there and got used to Lulu walking, it was kind of fun."

"Seriously?" Kate could barely keep from jumping up and down. "Awesome! So you'll keep working here and take a lesson next week?"

"Told you I'm not a quitter. But now comes the fun part. Watching Colt ride that horse with his long legs." Tori snorted a laugh. "I wish I'd thought to bring a camera so I could post it online."

Colt raised his hands and took a step back. "No way! I'm not riding that pony, and you aren't taking a picture. Ever."

"Sorry, young man," Mrs. Sorenson said firmly. "Barn rules. Anyone under the age of fourteen rides Lulu first, if they haven't taken lessons here before—or unless you bring a note from a previous trainer. We'll evaluate you and move you up to a full-size horse if you do well, but it's Lulu or nothing."

Colt's face was a picture of tragedy, and Tori and Kate burst into laughter.

"Fine." He gave in. "But I'm not riding English. I need to switch to a Western saddle."

Tori leaned close to Kate's ear. "This might be more fun than I realized. And next week I'm bringing my camera for sure."

Colt scowled as he grabbed Lulu's reins. "Next week I will not be riding this midget. Guaranteed. So you can leave your camera at home."

Kate and Tori kept a close eye on Colt as he walked, trotted, and cantered Lulu around the circle. Mrs. Sorenson hadn't even made him work on the lunge line the first few minutes, as he'd assured her he owned a horse and it wasn't necessary. His scowl had turned to triumph when the instructor asked him to put Lulu into a lope, and he'd done so with ease.

Mrs. Sorenson nodded. "Good job. Now bring her back to a walk and put her into a lope on her inside lead. Do you know how to do that?"

"I think so." He reined the mare to a walk and after several paces gave her a light bump with his heel. Lulu broke into a lope without hesitation.

Tori whispered to Kate, "Do you know what she meant?"

"No idea. A lope and a canter are the same thing, but people who ride Western call it a *lope*, and English riders a *canter*. That's all I know. Maybe she'll explain."

Mrs. Sorenson glanced their way. "Do you see how Lulu's inside leg is reaching farther ahead on every stride?"

Kate and Tori nodded.

"She's leading with that leg. Every horse has one lead they favor more than the other, so if you go one direction, it's pretty easy to get them to take the correct lead and more work going the other direction. Lulu's well-enough trained that she picks up either pretty easily, but Colt will have to ask her the correct way when we reverse directions, since this is the lead she prefers." She waved her hand in the air. "Pull her down and reverse, Colt."

"Wow." Tori bumped Kate's shoulder. "I guess I'm not going to be able to harass Colt anymore after this. He's pretty good."

"No kidding." Kate kept her gaze locked on the young man as he headed Lulu the other direction, wondering if she'd ever be that good a rider. She'd figured that because she'd taken some lessons in Spokane, she'd know more than Tori or Colt, but now she felt foolish. She didn't even sit a trot well, much less know how to post. She'd only cantered a time or two and had no idea how to get a horse on the correct lead. Colt could do it going either direction, from the way Lulu was responding now. Maybe it was because he owned a horse and got to ride all the time. Her thoughts drifted away from the action in the arena and returned to the chestnut mare in the paddock only blocks from home.

The door to the arena rolled open, and a middle-aged woman led in an unsaddled horse. She carried a long whip and had a lunge line attached to the halter, but she kept the horse at the other end so she wouldn't interfere with Colt and Lulu. On the far side of the arena, two college-aged girls opened a stall door, their voices drifting across to Kate.

"It's getting busy," Tori told Kate. "I guess more people work their horses on Saturday than during the week."

"Hi, you guys." Carissa Spencer, the girl who exercised clients' horses, walked up the alleyway toward them. "Are you taking your lessons?"

Kate nodded. "We're both finished, and it's Colt's turn. He's not too happy about riding a pony with his long legs." She snickered. "But he's doing such a good job, we won't be able to tease him about it." She glanced into the arena. "I thought my legs hung a long way below Lulu's belly, but Colt is an inch or so taller than me. Tori's a great fit for her, though, since she's not as tall as me or Colt." She looked back at Carissa. "Are you exercising a horse this morning?"

"Yep. Rocket." She held up a halter and lead rope. "I'm headed out to get him from the pasture. Want to come along?"

"Sure!" Both Kate and Tori spoke at the same time.

"Do you want to wait for your friend?" Carissa tipped her head toward Colt, who had slowed Lulu to a trot.

"Naw," Kate said. "He's been showing us up pretty bad, but he's almost done. I'd love to see the horses out in the pastures."

"Me too." Tori edged closer to Kate. "As long as we don't have to catch any and lead them in."

Carissa appeared surprised for a minute, but then she smiled. "You'll get used to doing that soon enough. I'll work with you if you'd like, on the days you come to clean stalls."

Tori's face brightened. "That would be awesome, thanks! We should let Mrs. Sorenson know we're leaving."

Tori slipped through the gate into the arena and caught the instructor's attention, then explained their errand.

Mrs. Sorenson motioned them on. "You girls did a good job today, both of you. See you next Saturday."

They followed Carissa down the alleyway and waved at Colt when he looked their direction.

Carissa swung open the people door at the far end and stepped into the bright April sunshine. She shaded her eyes with her hand and then pointed. "The pasture is on the other side of the twenty acres the barn owns, so we'll need to hike for a bit to reach the fence." She opened a gate and waited for Kate and Tori to pass, then closed it.

Kate took in the scattering of fir trees that dotted the pasture in the distance, giving the horses shade, and then gestured toward the large outdoor arena not far away. "Why do they have one outside when there's a perfectly good one indoors?"

Carissa peered toward the outdoor arena. "It gets pretty busy in the late spring, summer, and fall. Once the outdoor arena completely dries out, a lot of our clients prefer to work outside. We set up jumps on one end of this arena and cavalletti poles on the other."

Tori scrunched her brows. "Cava-what?"

Carissa waved at the stack of poles lying on the ground outside the arena. "You place those poles on short stands a certain distance apart and walk your horse over them, then trot, then canter. It's the beginning training step to teaching a horse to jump, or to teach a student how to guide a horse over obstacles."

"Oh." Tori moistened her lips. "I think I'll pass. Staying on at a walk is enough."

Carissa laughed. "You might not feel that way after you've ridden awhile. It gets in your blood and can be quite addictive, once you understand what you're doing and get the hang of riding."

Tori didn't seem convinced. "Maybe, but I still don't think I want to learn to jump or even walk over cava-whatever-they-are."

Kate stifled a giggle. "Cavalletti. And I'd love to learn to jump. It's one of the things I've always wanted to do."

Carissa struck off along a path leading to a pasture fenced with white boards. "Rocket is in this pasture. He was turned out last night, since he's been cooped up in a stall for a couple of days. We let them out so they don't get barn sour or start cribbing." She looked at Tori. "That means they chew and suck on wood when they get bored. Thoroughbreds tend to do it more than some breeds, and we don't want Rocket to start a bad habit."

She placed her fingers to her lips and let loose with a shrill whistle, then removed a bag of apple treats from her jacket pocket. "We'll get more than Rocket, since we reward them with treats when they come. Sure saves a lot of running around the pasture trying to catch them."

A small herd of a half-dozen horses galloped toward them, a mix of bays and chestnuts, but Kate didn't see a gray. "Where's Rocket?"

Carissa shaded her eyes and waited, then blasted the whistle again. All of a sudden the big gray horse appeared in the distance, running at a fast gallop.

Kate and Tori stared, their mouths hanging open. Kate grabbed Tori's arm, yanking her away from the fence. "He's not going to stop! He's going to crash into the fence!"

Carissa planted herself in the way and waved her arms. "Rocket. Whoa, boy!"

The gelding didn't slow but veered ever so slightly from where Carissa stood. Three strides from the fence, he seemed to gather himself, and in the next stride he leaped into the air, sailing over the top rail. He landed on the other side and galloped down the path that led toward the barn, with Carissa racing after him.

Chapter Sixteen

Kate and Tori sprinted after Carissa, weaving their way around the corner of the outdoor arena and jumping over a couple of poles that rolled away from the stack.

"Rocket sure lived up to his name when he jumped that fence," Kate told Tori as they ran. "I hope Carissa can catch him before he gets to the road."

"Yeah, me too." Tori slowed to a jog when they reached the end of the barn.

Kate pointed. "Look, he's coming this way." The big gray had circled the barn and slowed from a gallop to a fast trot, his head lifted and nostrils flaring as he moved toward them.

Tori shrank against the barn wall. "What should we do? We can't catch him, and I don't want to get trampled."

Kate didn't move. She lifted her arms out to the side. "It's okay, Rocket. Calm down, boy."

Carissa skidded to a halt behind the horse. "Good job, Kate. Stand there and don't move, and keep your hands out like that." She moved toward the gelding, her voice low and soothing. "Come on, Rocket. Here's an apple treat." The halter and lead were still slung over her arm, but her other hand was extended with a treat on her palm.

Rocket snorted and sidestepped as she approached, then took off again, tossing his head. He trotted toward the large out-door arena, each step a thing of beauty as he arched his neck and pranced. Kate was so taken with how pretty he was, she almost forgot to worry about the horse.

Mrs. Wilder ran from the barn with Mrs. Sorenson and Colt right behind her. Colt, eyes wide, drew to a stop only feet from Kate and Tori. "What happened? How did Rocket get loose?"

Kate swung her gaze to his. "You should have seen him. It was awesome! Carissa called the horses in, and Rocket came at a full gallop. He jumped the pasture fence like it wasn't even there."

"Nice! I wish I would've been there." Colt rubbed his hands together and grinned. "I've never jumped a horse and don't want to learn, but it's still fun to see them do it."

Tori groaned. "It wasn't fun at all. I thought he was going to run into the fence where we were standing and kill us, and then he sailed over close to our heads. I'm never learning to jump."

"I want to." Kate breathed the words almost like a prayer. "I can't think of anything that would be more fun."

Rocket acted as though he were playing a game as he evaded the women's attempts to catch him, and once again he headed toward the barn at a fast trot.

Colt jerked his head. "Come on! We'll go around the other way and see if we can head him off. The driveway leading to the road is just past the barn, and he could get hit."

All three of them took off at a run, and Kate caught sight of the adults headed the other direction. Maybe they could stop him with their combined efforts.

But when Kate, Tori, and Colt rounded the far corner, Kate sucked in a hard breath. "Oh no!"

Rocket was headed toward the road, and a pickup was traveling toward them too fast to stop! If Rocket tried to run across, he could get killed and possibly cause a horrible accident.

Colt kicked into high gear and tore out ahead of the girls, down the short gravel driveway. He ran to Rocket's left, waving his arms and shouting. The horse skidded to a stop in the loose gravel and snorted, his neck arched and ears pricked forward. Kate and Tori moved up beside Colt, their arms extended to the side, and the three slowly moved forward as one unit.

Kate dropped her voice to a low croon. "Easy, Rocket. You don't want to go out in the road. Come on, boy. Easy now." The pickup zipped past, and Kate almost cried with relief. Now if someone could catch Rocket before any other cars came.

Carissa stopped a few feet away. "Good job, guys. I think he's done running now, aren't you, boy?" She held her hand out, again offering the apple treat. Rocket sniffed the air, then moved forward, his lips working. Carissa pulled her hand a little closer to her side but kept the treat visible. As the horse took another step and reached for the treat, she slipped the end of the rope around his neck. "Gotcha! You've had your fun, you rascal. Time to go back inside."

Kate, Tori, and Colt held still until Carissa had the halter secured. Then they relaxed.

As Carissa headed back to the barn with the gelding, Mrs. Wilder's worried expression disappeared behind a wide smile. "Thank you, kids. I'm not sure we'd have caught him if it hadn't been for your quick thinking. I definitely made the right decision when I hired you three. You can hang around if you want to or head home. I need to get back inside, but I'll see you next Tuesday."

Kate glanced at Tori. Her friend was shaking so hard, it looked like she might fall over. "Hey, what's wrong?"

Tori took two steps and sank onto a large rock positioned on the side of the driveway. "I can't believe we did that."

"Did what?" Kate stopped beside Tori and glanced at Colt, who shrugged.

"Stood in the path of that horse. He could have run over the top of us."

Colt grinned. "Yeah, pretty exciting, huh?"

Tori glared. "No! It was scary, not exciting."

"Well, we lived through it, and Rocket didn't get hurt. I'd say that's what matters, right?" Colt's smile faded, and his voice softened. "Were you really scared?"

Tori heaved a sigh. "I guess not when it was happening. It was kind of exciting knowing I helped keep him safe. It hit me after Carissa caught him and Mrs. Wilder thanked us."

"See?" Colt spread his arms wide. "You're going to make a first-rate horsewoman. You did the right thing when you were needed. Doesn't matter that you got shook up later. That's normal."

Kate grabbed Tori's hand and tugged her to her feet. "Colt is right. It might be a good idea if you don't say too much to your mom about what happened today—or maybe don't tell her you were scared. She might worry."

Tori nodded. "Right. I guess no one got hurt. But I think I'm ready to be done with the barn and head home."

Chapter Seventeen

Kate kicked at a rock on the edge of the road. Tori walked beside her in silence as they pushed their bikes down the short drive to the main road. Tori hadn't suggested they ride, and Kate was waiting for her friend to explain what she meant about being done with the barn.

Minutes dragged and felt like hours. Still Tori didn't speak. Finally Kate couldn't stand it. "Are you quitting?"

Tori stopped and stared. "Quitting what?"

Kate gripped her bike handles hard. "Working at the barn."

"No. What makes you say that?"

"You said you were ready to be done with the barn and head home, and since then you haven't spoken a word. I know how scared you were when Rocket jumped the fence, and I don't blame you. I'm not gonna be mad if you quit."

Tori's eyes widened. "I wasn't even thinking of quitting, Kate. I was thinking about what happened, yeah, but mostly about what Colt said. That I got scared when it was over, not while it was happening. I did the right thing. I pushed past my fear and helped you guys keep Rocket from running into the road and causing an accident. That felt pretty amazing."

Kate gaped for a moment before she realized her mouth was hanging open. "Wow. Seriously?"

"Seriously." Tori nodded.

Kate shut her eyes in relief. "I'm glad. And yeah, it was pretty amazing. Want to stop by and see my mare?"

Tori arched her brow. "Your mare?"

Kate laughed. "Sorry. I guess I've been calling her that in my head because I wish she were mine. The one we found that's thin. I've only stopped over there once since Pete ran away. I'd like to see if there's any sign of hay in that shelter again. If not, I'm going to beg my dad to figure out who owns her or call the sheriff. I wish someone lived in that old house next to her pen so we could ask."

"I know. My dad hasn't had any luck finding out who owns her either." Tori swung her leg over her bike. "Let's head over there. It would be so cool if you could get her, Kate. You guys have your own barn and pasture, and you even have a saddle and bridle. Have you asked your parents if you could buy her if you find the owner?"

Kate pedaled her bike harder and kept pace with Tori. "They aren't too hot on the idea, but I'm going to ask them again after

Dad's been working a little longer. The grass is coming up in our pasture, and we wouldn't need to feed her much hay until next winter. She'd need grain and vitamins and her feet trimmed, though. I wish I had a paying job so I could help."

They slowed as they neared the paddock where the mare lived. Kate propped her bike against a tree, and Tori laid hers on the ground. The chestnut mare trotted across the enclosure and whinnied. She stopped at the fence and stretched her neck toward the girls.

Kate laughed. "She remembers us!"

Tori rolled her eyes. "I think it's more likely she remembers the carrots. Did you bring any?"

Kate nodded. "I always have some in my backpack, in case. I haven't been able to get over here for a few days, though, so they're not going to be fresh."

"I doubt she'll care. She's pacing the fence waiting. She looks a little better, don't you think?" Tori moved toward the paddock but cast a glance over her shoulder at Kate.

"Yeah, she does. Her ribs aren't showing as much, but her feet are still terrible. There are pieces of hay on the ground in the lean-to, so I guess the owner must have decided to feed her more often. Maybe somebody turned him in for starving her."

"He deserves it, if you ask me." Tori stroked the mare's face. "Poor thing. I'm glad you're feeling better, girl."

Kate dropped her backpack on the ground and held the bag of carrots toward Tori. "Grab some. We'll take turns. Even if she's getting hay, she'll still appreciate treats."

They passed the next minutes in silence as the mare munched the carrots and then sniffed their hands and arms for more.

A crunch of gravel caused the girls to spin in time to see a four-door sedan pull in off the road and park several yards away. A white-haired man who appeared older than Kate's grandpa pushed open the door. Glancing at the horse, he shut the car door and headed toward Kate and Tori. "May I help you girls with something?"

Kate's heart lurched. *This must be the owner of the house, and we're trespassing. Will he call the sheriff? Have we done the wrong thing by stopping to feed the skinny horse?* "Uh, no, we don't need any help. We came to feed her carrots." She nodded at the mare, then gestured toward the house. "Do you live here?"

Sudden anger flared. If this man was supposed to be taking care of the horse, he'd done a lousy job. He was the one who should be ashamed of himself, not her and Tori.

He halted a yard or so away. "May I ask your names?"

Kate narrowed her eyes, not missing the fact that he hadn't answered her question or introduced himself. Her parents always told her not to talk to strangers. She shot a warning glance to Tori and began to edge toward the tree where she'd propped her bike. "We need to leave now. Sorry. We don't know you, and we can't stay. Our parents are expecting us home."

Tori nodded. "Yeah. My dad is probably looking for us right now."

The man gave a gentle smile. "My name is Harold Miller, and no, I don't own this house or live here. My home is in Hood River."

Kate kept edging toward her bike. "Then why are *you* here, and why are you asking *us* questions?"

He took a step back and held up his hand. "I'm sorry if I scared you, girls. That wasn't my intention. I own this horse, and I'll probably move her out of here soon."

Chapter Eighteen

Kate felt as though she'd been kicked in the stomach and lost all her air. In fact, she felt close to losing her breakfast. This couldn't be true! She wanted to tell this man to go away and leave her horse alone. Maybe it wasn't true. Maybe he was lying and didn't even own the mare.

"If you own her, why haven't you been feeding her?" Kate insisted. "Why did you let her get so skinny and let her feet get so long and broken?"

A rush of red colored the man's cheeks. "I'm sorry to say I thought the person I hired to care for her was doing a good job."

Tori cocked her head. "So you never once came and checked on her? Didn't you want to know she was okay? When we first found her, she didn't have any hay at all, and she was awful hungry. That's cruelty to animals, you know."

Mr. Miller ducked his head and then looked up. "Yes, I know, and I feel bad about it. She belonged to my wife." His shoulders slumped.

Kate hesitated. She thought she spotted tears shining in his eyes when he spoke of his wife. "So … why doesn't your wife take care of her? Is she sick?"

"No." He swallowed hard. "She went on to heaven ahead of me last fall. Capri was the last horse Nora owned. She sold her other two but held on to Capri because she'd been such a good riding horse. They won several hunter-jumper competitions together."

Kate gaped. "Your wife jumped her?"

The man chuckled. "My wife was ten years younger than me. Don't let this hair fool you. Nora was only fifty-eight when cancer took her, and she was fit as a fiddle and very athletic right up until the time she took sick. Capri hasn't been used this last year or so, but Nora always enjoyed riding her."

"Wow." Kate breathed the word. "She's a Thoroughbred, right?"

"Yes, although she's not registered. I should have come over and checked on her through the winter, but the man I was paying assured me he'd bought the best hay, had several bags of grain and vitamins, and was having the farrier over on a regular basis to care for her feet. I paid him well and assumed he was honest."

Kate walked back to the paddock and stroked Capri under her forelock. "How'd you figure out he wasn't doing his job? Tori and I have been coming over for a few weeks now, and we didn't see any sign of hay at all at first. My dad was going to turn her in to the sheriff if she didn't have any food the next time we came, but there was some in the lean-to the last couple of times."

"I'm afraid I know very little about horses. I called the man a couple of weeks ago and asked for a receipt for her hay. I'm guessing that might be when he finally purchased some and started feeding her. When I questioned him, he told me he didn't want to continue, that it was too much bother."

Tori frowned. "That's rotten! Why'd he take the job in the first place if he didn't want to do it?"

Mr. Miller shrugged. "I suppose he thought it was easy money, and he could get by with doing very little. When he realized I wasn't checking on Capri, he slacked off. It was my responsibility, and I should have stayed on top of it. I guess I was having a hard time and didn't think." He leaned an elbow against a rail of the fence. "I appreciate you girls coming to check on her, but you won't have to worry about Capri any longer."

Kate's stomach knotted. Mr. Miller's tone hadn't sounded like good news was coming. "Why's that?"

"I've made arrangements to take her to the livestock auction in The Dalles at the end of the week. I'm not set up to care for her, and she needs to go to a new home. I held on to her for as long as I did for Nora's sake, but it's not fair to her to continue."

Kate straightened. "My dad wouldn't be able to buy her, but she could live at our place. We have a big barn and pasture, and I love her."

"That's very kind," Mr. Miller said firmly, "but I've made up my mind. I don't want the ongoing responsibility of owning a horse. She's going to be sold next Saturday."

Kate and Tori watched Mr. Miller climb into his car and drive off. Kate couldn't believe they'd found out who owned Capri and that they might lose her, all in the same day. "We can't let this happen."

Tori stared at her. "What?"

"We can't let Mr. Miller take Capri to the auction to sell her."

"Why not? At least she'll get fed if she goes to a new home. That's a good thing, right?" Tori absently stroked the mare's neck.

"No, it isn't. There's no way to tell if the people who buy her will feed her or starve her too. And what's worse, she might end up going for dog food." Kate slapped the top bar of the fence, and Capri snorted and bolted backward. "Oops, sorry, girl." Kate held out her hand and allowed the mare to sniff it. "I didn't mean to scare you."

Tori frowned. "What do you mean, dog food? That's a weird thing to say."

"Didn't you know that a lot of horses at auctions get sold to meat plants?"

"No. That's awful!"

"Yeah, it is. There aren't nearly as many meat plants now, 'cause lots of them got shut down, but it still happens. Whole truckloads of horses get purchased and hauled to Canada for slaughter. There are so many horses for sale now, and tons of people don't have the money to buy them or even care for the ones they own. I've heard news stories about it, and I researched it online once. It made me sick."

Tori's eyes widened. "You think that could happen to Capri? But Mr. Miller said his wife loved her. I don't think he'd want that to happen to his wife's horse."

"He also said he doesn't know much about horses, and he's hoping she'll go to a new home. That would probably happen if she was all shed out, her weight was up, and her feet were trimmed. It would even be better if someone could ride her when they put her up for bid, so people knew she was broke.

But if they just run her into the sales arena and start bidding, there's a good chance she'll sell for meat prices."

"What can we do? It's not like either of us has the money to buy her."

"I know." Defeat washed over Kate, making her want to cry in frustration. "Let's go home and talk to my dad. Maybe he'll have an idea. No way do I want Capri to die."

Chapter Nineteen

Kate didn't know whether to beg or cry or holler, but somehow she doubted any of those would convince her father to change his mind. Too bad Tori hadn't wanted to stay, but she understood why her friend would feel weird about trying to help Kate talk to her parents. Dad stood like a block of stone in the living room, with only his warm eyes showing his sorrow.

Kate twisted her hands together. "There's got to be a way to save her, Dad." She turned to her other parent. "Mom? You owned horses years ago. You know what could happen to Capri if she's sent to the auction."

Mom nodded. "I do. But I also know she could end up getting a good home. My dad bought more than one horse at the auction yard. Most of the people who attend are there to buy a horse for their ranch or family, not to buy one for the packing plant."

Kate scowled, still not convinced. "But why take that chance? She was a champion hunter-jumper. She deserves to go to a good home."

"I'm sure Mr. Miller will tell the auction people about Capri's history, Kate. He'll want to get the best possible price for her," Mom said.

Dad sank onto the couch next to Mom. "It's not our business, honey. Capri belongs to Mr. Miller. If he decides that's what is best, it's not up to us to question his decision."

Kate spread her arms wide. "But we could buy her!"

Dad shut his eyes. "We've discussed this before, Kate. I'm not going through it again. I'm sorry."

"But Dad!"

"No more argument, Kate. You need to take care of your chores. I don't want your work at the barn to interfere with your responsibilities at home. You promised to keep up, remember?"

"Yeah." She scuffed her toe against the carpet, wanting to say more but knowing she shouldn't. When Dad used that tone, any discussion was over. Finished. Done with. Nothing would change his mind. Not even an earthquake.

Pete came into the room, twisting his fingers together. "Kate is sad?"

Kate tried to smile, but it didn't feel real. "I'm okay, buddy. Don't worry."

He edged closer, his fingers still in motion. "Kate wants her horse. Pete wants Kate to have her horse. Pete likes Kate's horse."

Mom walked over to Pete, then looked at Kate's father. "We need to be careful what we talk about in front of little ears. Remember what happened the last time he got worried about Kate's horse."

"Right." Dad pushed to his feet and extended his hand. "Want me to read to you, Peter?"

Pete stared at his toes, which dipped and rocked. "Guess so. Pete likes horses too."

"I know. Come on. We'll find a book about horses."

Pete dipped one shoulder. "No. Read *Pete's Dragon*. Pete likes dragons too."

Dad chuckled. "You've got it. Dragons it is."

Kate watched them leave, then pleaded with her mother. "Can't you convince Dad to change his mind? He listens to you."

Her mother raised her brows. "You know better than that, Kate. If your father says no, then that's where we leave it."

"But you don't agree. I know you don't. I saw it in your expression when we were talking about it." Kate didn't care if she sounded upset. She *was* upset. This wasn't a bit fair.

Her mother put her arm around Kate's waist and drew her close. "I understand what you're feeling and going through, honey. That's what you saw on my face. I care that you're hurting. But I also get what your father is saying. It's not that we don't love you or want you to have your dream. We're trying to be careful with our money right now, that's all. I'm not saying it won't ever happen. Maybe in a year or so we can think about buying a horse."

Kate stiffened. "Capri might be dead by then. Even if she's not, someone else will own her."

"I know that, but believe it or not, she's not the only horse in the world. There are others—nice ones you'll like just as much. You simply need to be patient."

"Patience is overrated." Kate grumbled the words she'd heard her dad say one time in the past. But she knew Mom was right and she was the one not being fair. "I'm sorry, Mom. I know you guys aren't rich. It's just that I want Capri so bad."

Kate shrugged into her backpack on Tuesday afternoon and followed Tori to where they'd left their bikes outside the barn where they worked. She loved her job, but she couldn't quit thinking about Capri and the fact that the horse she'd come to care about was going to be hauled to the auction and might be sold for dog food. She shuddered, not wanting to even think about the possibility. If only she could come up with a way to purchase the mare. Maybe they could attend the auction and pray she went supercheap.

Tori swung her leg over her bike and stared at Kate, who gripped her handlebars and didn't move. "Are you coming? What's wrong with you? You've been spaced out all day."

Kate mounted her bike. "I know. Sorry for being a dweeb. I can't get my mind off Capri, that's all."

"Hey, I hear you. I'm worried about her too, and I don't even want her for my own horse." Tori made a face. "I wish your parents would change their minds about getting her for you."

"Not likely." Kate propped her foot on one pedal but kept the other on the ground. "Want to ride over there on the way home? I brought carrots and some apple slices. Who knows? It might be one of our last chances to see her."

"Sure. Let's go." Tori pushed ahead down the driveway, and Kate followed.

They rounded the last corner, and Kate peered ahead, anxious to see Capri shove her nose across the fence, eager for treats. But she didn't see the mare standing at the edge of the paddock. Maybe she was in the lean-to eating some of the plentiful hay Mr. Miller made sure she was getting now that he'd taken over her care. Kate pedaled harder. Mom would be expecting her home for supper soon, and she still had homework to finish before tomorrow.

They slid to a stop near the pen, and Kate dumped her bike, not even caring that it hit the ground too hard. "Where is she?"

Tori bolted to the rails and peered inside. "She's gone. Do you think Mr. Miller already came and got her? It's kind of weird he left the gate open, but I guess if there's no horse to escape, it doesn't matter."

Kate slapped her open palm against the top board. "I can't believe this! He said he was going to take her this weekend. We didn't even get a chance to say good-bye!"

Chapter Twenty

Kate burst through the door of her house and raced to the kitchen. "Capri is gone, Mom! Mr. Miller must have picked her up early to take her to the auction. I'm sick. She's going to be sold for meat, I just know it." She clenched her jaws to keep from saying something she shouldn't or, worse yet, bursting into tears. But if there were ever a time when she didn't care if she was a sissy and cried, this was it.

Mom leaned against the counter by the sink, where she'd been scrubbing a skillet, and faced Kate. "I'm so sorry, honey. You didn't get to see her before she left?"

"No. And it's not fair."

Her mother came over and wrapped her arms around Kate's shoulders, pulling her close. "Sweetie, lots of things in life aren't fair, but I understand why this hurts."

Kate absorbed the love of her mom's embrace for a minute, then shifted. "Thanks, Mom. Do you think Dad would be willing to let me attend the auction?"

"I don't think that's a wise idea. It will only make losing her that much harder."

"You mean because I might find out she didn't go to a good home? But maybe she'd go really cheap, and we could buy her." She gazed at her mom and tried to put all the pleading she could into her gaze. "Please? Talk to Dad?"

Mom sighed. "You need to let it go, Kate."

Dad came to the doorway. "Let what go?"

Kate ran to him and poured out the entire story again. "So can we go to the auction, Dad? Please?"

He started to answer, but the phone rang in the living room, cutting him off. "Just a sec." He walked into the other room and returned a short while later. "That was a Mr. Miller. He says he met Kate and Tori a few days ago when he stopped to check on his mare. He wanted to know if the girls came to visit Capri earlier today." He looked at Kate with a questioning gaze. "You said you did, right?"

"Yeah. But I told you, she was gone." Kate saw her dad shoot Mom a concerned look. "What's going on? Why did he call to see if we came over? Mr. Miller said he didn't mind if we fed her carrots, but we didn't even get a chance to do that today."

Dad placed two fingers under Kate's chin and lifted her face until she was gazing right into his eyes. "So you two girls didn't go over on your way to the barn to pet her or feed her?"

"No way, Dad. We went right to work and stopped there on our way home. Why?"

"Because he stopped there late this afternoon to check on her. The gate was open, and she was gone. You're the only people he knows, other than the man who was supposed to care for her, who's ever shown an interest in Capri, so he thought you might have gotten spooked that he was selling her and let her out."

"John! I hope you told him what Kate said, and that she and Tori would never do something like that."

Gratitude welled in Kate's heart. Her mother believed her. Did Dad? She studied his calm face and waited for his response.

"Of course I did, Nan. In fact, I told him that Kate came home quite upset and disappointed that the mare was gone and assumed Mr. Miller had already picked her up for transport to the auction. He was relieved and disappointed at the same time, as the girls were his only lead."

Kate clenched her hands into fists. "So where is she if he didn't pick her up? Did someone steal her? I can't believe this is happening. We've got to help find her!"

Kate woke early the next morning with a stomachache. She didn't think she'd slept more than three hours, since she'd worried about Capri most of the night. It had been dark thirty minutes or so after Mr. Miller called, and there had been nothing her family could do to help find her. Kate wanted to drive around the entire area and shine their car's headlights into every pasture, but Dad said no.

She kicked off her blankets and bolted from bed. It was only six o'clock, and she had a full hour before she needed to get ready for school—more if she hurried. She threw on her clothes and headed for the stairs. If Mom and Dad weren't up yet, maybe she could leave them a note that she planned to ride her bike and search for Capri. Surely they wouldn't mind her doing that!

She tiptoed down the stairs. Rufus needed to go outside, and if nothing else, she could look around while taking him for a short walk.

She stepped into the kitchen. Dad was snapping the leash on Rufus, who stood there with a big doggy grin, his tail thumping against the cupboard doors. "Hi, Dad."

His brows rose in surprise. "What are you doing up so early? Don't you have another hour or so before you get ready for school?"

"Yeah, but I couldn't sleep."

"Worried about Capri, huh?" Dad gave her a sad smile.

"Uh-huh. Can I take Rufus for his walk?"

Dad hesitated for a second. "I suppose, but I have time before I leave for work. You sure you want to do it?"

She nodded. "I want to look for Capri."

"Honey, it's not likely you'll find her. She could be anywhere. I'd hate to see you get your hopes up." He kept a firm grip on Rufus's leash.

"I know, but I have to try. Please?" She held out her hand and waited.

Finally he gave her the lead. "I need to go to work early, so I might be gone by the time you get back. Your mom had a bad headache last night, so don't wake her when you get home if she's not up, okay?"

"Sure, Dad. Thanks." Kate lifted her hand in farewell and headed to the door. She had no idea what she'd do if she didn't find Capri. It made her sick thinking about the mare wandering around lost, but another part of her rejoiced that the horse had gotten loose. Maybe somehow she'd escape going to the auction this way, and Kate would still have a chance to make Capri her own.

Thirty minutes later, Kate checked her watch again, wishing for the hundredth time that she didn't have to go to school today. She'd seen plenty of horses on the mile or so of road she'd covered, but not the chestnut mare she longed to find.

"Come on, Rufus. Time to turn around." She tugged on the dog's leash, pulling him away from sniffing along the side of the road. "We'll take a shortcut across this field and come out at the back of our barn." She shivered and tugged her collar up to protect her neck from the early morning chill, wishing she'd grabbed a stocking hat.

Rufus resisted the tug for several seconds, then finally gave in and followed as she struck out across the field, covered by ankle-high grass and weeds. Dad would be gone by now, and she'd need to hurry to get ready for school. Maybe she'd ride her bike to give herself a few more minutes. It was a good thing she didn't wear much makeup—only a little lip gloss and a touch of mascara—or it would take her twice as long.

Rufus trotted ahead of her, straining at the leash. He hadn't been fed yet this morning, and he probably wanted to get back to the kitchen and his food dish.

Kate increased her pace to keep up. "I'm coming. Calm down, okay?"

He gave a short yip and pulled harder.

The back of their barn was in sight, and Kate thought she saw something move along the far wall. She put her hand above her eyes to block the morning sun. "Do you see something, boy?" She gripped the leash tighter, not liking the idea of running into a stray dog. Rufus was gentle with people, but he had a protective streak when it came to other dogs on his property.

They reached the end of the barn, and Kate slowed her pace, wondering if she should go down the opposite side from where she'd seen the movement. The last thing she wanted was Rufus in a dog fight. A crunch of gravel sounded, and Kate halted, the hair on her arms standing on end. *That must be a pretty big dog to make that much noise.*

Rufus barked again and strained at his leash. Kate gave a hard yank. "Down, Rufus. Leave it." The dog relaxed, but only slightly, his body still quivering.

Kate stood still, not sure what to do. She hated to wake Mom if she had a headache, but it sounded like something was trying to get into their barn. Maybe the same people who stole the saddles from Mrs. Wilder's barn thought there was something worth stealing here. She almost laughed thinking how shocked they'd be at finding nothing but junk inside.

Then she sobered. Someone breaking into their barn wasn't anything to joke about. She sucked in her breath.

At that instant something struck the corner of the barn behind her with a soft *thunk*. Kate froze, then slowly pivoted and stared.

Several yards away, Capri munched on a straggle of moldy hay she must have found near the side door. Kate wanted to do a happy dance, but if she did, the mare would probably bolt and run like Rocket had.

Rufus sniffed the air, and his hackles went down. He dropped his head and whined, probably wondering what this large creature was that had invaded his space. Kate patted the dog. "Good boy. Quiet, now."

She bent over and yanked a handful of grass growing next to the wall; then she eased forward, her hand extended. "Hey there, girl. You remember me, right? Come on, have some grass." She kept her voice soft and didn't make any sudden movements, praying the mare would be more interested in eating than running away.

Capri raised her head. She took a step forward and then froze. A shiver ran over her body, and she backed up a couple of steps. Kate scanned the pasture, wondering what could have spooked her, but didn't see anything nearby. "Easy, girl. It's just grass. You're hungry, right?" Keeping her hand extended, she eased ahead inch by inch.

"That's right. There you go." Kate wanted to shout for joy as Capri moved toward her and nibbled at the grass, then dropped her head and checked the ground for anything that might have fallen.

Kate unsnapped the leash from Rufus. "Stay, boy. Sit." The big dog sat and stared at her, tail thumping. "Good boy."

She stroked the mare's neck, then slid the leash around her and clipped it. "Whew! I've got you! Come on, let's get in the barn. I'm sure glad I cleaned out a couple of stalls, and there's some clean hay in the loft, even if it's old. You'll be safe here until I can decide what to do."

Chapter Twenty-One

Kate barely got through the day without exploding. She'd kept her word and not awakened her mom, but then she'd felt guilty all day that she hadn't told anyone about finding Capri. Other than Tori, of course. She hadn't had a chance to talk to Tori privately before school, as Kate barely made it before the first bell rang, so she told her friend at lunch break.

Tori's happy face was exactly what Kate had hoped for, but then her friend had turned serious. "So what are you going to do?"

"What do you mean?" Kate frowned.

"I mean, you didn't tell your mom or call Mr. Miller before you came to school. Isn't that gonna seem kinda weird?"

Kate squirmed, not liking where this conversation seemed to be headed. "She's safe in our barn. I even found some hay to feed her, and she's in a clean stall."

Tori stared at her. "You *are* going to tell Mr. Miller, right?"

Kate sighed. "Yeah. I mean, it's not like I have a choice. But …"

"But what?" Tori tapped the toe of her shoe while she waited for an answer.

"I was thinking maybe I could wait a day or two, and then it would be too late to take her to the auction." As soon as the words left her mouth, she almost cringed. Swiftly she held up her palm to shut out Tori's wide eyes. "All right, all right, I didn't mean it." She paused. "Well, I guess I did mean it, but I won't do it. I'd like to, 'cause it might save her life, but I know it's wrong. I suppose I'll tell Mom as soon as I get home, and then I'll call Mr. Miller. At least I got to see her again before she gets sold."

Tori nodded, her eyes soft and sympathetic. "Yeah. It is wrong to keep it a secret. You're doing the right thing, Kate, even if it's hard."

Kate hung up the phone and tried to be strong. Mr. Miller would be over in an hour or so to pick up Capri. She thought she'd talked herself into accepting the fact that the mare had to leave, but this was harder than she'd expected.

Her mom stepped close and hugged Kate. "I'm proud of you, honey."

Kate pressed her face into her mother's shoulder. "I thought you'd be so mad at me for not telling you sooner. I'm sorry, Mom." She pulled away. "I wanted to tell you this morning, and then I started thinking that maybe I could keep her hidden for a couple of days, and no one would know. I could tell you guys after the auction was over, and it would save Capri's life."

Mom ran her fingers through Kate's long curls. "But you knew it was wrong."

"Yeah. And then I saw the look on Tori's face when I hinted at it, and I knew I couldn't do it. I wanted to, something fierce, but you and Dad would have been upset and disappointed, and I didn't want that either."

"Why don't you go to the barn and spend some time with Capri before Mr. Miller comes? Dad or I will come get you when it's time." She opened the refrigerator and withdrew an apple. "Here, she'd probably like this."

"Thanks, Mom." Kate gave her mother a quick squeeze, then stepped toward the kitchen door, suddenly anxious to get out of the house and be with the horse she'd come to think of as her own. Now it would never happen, but there was nothing wrong with dreaming for this one last hour, was there?

A soft nicker greeted Kate as she walked down the alleyway toward the end stall where she'd put Capri. She slid open
the door and stepped inside, then shut it behind her. The mare
nuzzled her arm, then stretched toward the apple clutched in
Kate's hand. She laughed and held it out. "All right, greedy girl.
Take a bite." She gripped the apple so Capri could take a chunk
out of it, then held it out again. "One piece left." Kate held it on
the flat of her palm.

"I sure hope you'll get apples at your new home, girl." She
slid her arms around the mare's neck and hugged her. Capri
dropped her head and didn't move, seeming to sense Kate's distress. "I wish you could be mine. I tried to save you from the
auction, really I did. I'm going to pray that you get a good home
where the people will love you as much as I do."

The minutes raced by, and sooner than Kate expected, she
heard the outer door open and footsteps in the alleyway. "Dad?
Mom? Is Mr. Miller here?"

Both of her parents appeared at the door of Capri's stall,
their expressions serious. "Can you come out, Kate? We need to
talk to you."

She slid open the door and slipped out, then closed it behind
her, dread hitting her hard. "He wants to take her now, doesn't
he? It's okay, I'm ready." Kate worked to keep her voice steady,
but the last couple of words wavered.

Dad placed his hands on her shoulders and looked into her eyes. "First, I wish you had told your mother that you found Capri this morning or called me on my cell. That would've been better than waiting until after school."

Kate hung her head. "I know."

"Second," he said as he lifted her chin, "I told you not to wake your mom, so you aren't really to blame. And after talking to your mother, I understand a little better what you were going through. Now, we have something to tell you about Mr. Miller."

Kate almost forgot to breathe as she stared at her father. "What?"

"He was very grateful you found Capri. We talked for a long time, and he's feeling pretty bad about taking her to the auction. He said it's not what his wife would have wanted to have happen to her favorite horse. When she got sick, she told him to find a good home for Capri—to make sure she went to someone who would love and care for her. He'd forgotten that promise in his grief over his wife's passing."

"So he's not going to take her to the auction? He's going to try to find a home for her instead?" She gripped her hands in front of her.

"Yes, he is. In fact, he already has." Dad released Kate's chin and smiled. "And she's not going anywhere. He decided that she belongs with you, along with the ton of hay he paid for that's sitting at the house of the man who was supposed to feed her. He's also going to send a farrier over to trim her feet and have the vet make sure she's wormed and up on all her shots for the year."

Kate gaped at him, but her brain felt as though it had fallen into an ice-cold lake and wouldn't work. "I don't understand. Why me?"

"He saw how much you love Capri when you and Tori were visiting her, and how you insisted she needed proper care and a good home. Plus, he was very impressed that you could have waited to tell him the truth about finding her until the auction had passed, but you called him instead."

Warmth rushed into Kate's cheeks. "I thought about not telling him. I wanted to wait and hide her until it was too late, so that's not something to be proud of."

Dad shook his head. "But you didn't. Mom told me you decided it was wrong. I told Mr. Miller about that. He said that's the kind of person his wife would have approved of and would want him to give Capri to. And I agree."

Kate looked from her father to her mother, barely able to hope. "Seriously? But you said it was too soon for me to have a horse—that they cost too much money, and I need to wait."

"I know what I said, but with Mr. Miller's offer of the hay, the farrier, and the vet to start things off, I think we can handle it. My probation period at work is finished, and my boss told me

I'll be getting a raise. I can't think of a better way to celebrate than for my girl to have her dream. One more thing." He held up his hand. "There won't be much in the way of a Christmas present the end of this year, other than the things we need to care for Capri. Are you good with that?"

Kate threw her arms around him. "*Way* good! I can't believe it! Thank you both! Oh, wow, I want to call Tori!" Something else hit her. "Where's Pete? He needs to know what's going on. He's going to be so happy that I got my horse. Can I teach him to ride, Mom?"

Mom shook her head. "One thing at a time. I think you should take a few lessons on Capri first and make sure you can handle her properly. You won't be riding her without supervision for a while, but I think eventually we might let Pete sit on her, with me or your dad close by." She hugged Kate. "And we wanted to tell you without Pete being here, so the excitement wouldn't be too much for him. We left him watching his *Pete's Dragon* DVD. How about we all go inside and tell him? Mr. Miller's having his son drop off the ton of hay this evening, as he wants to be sure Capri is properly fed."

"Whoopee!" Kate pumped her fist in the air. She couldn't wait to tell Pete and then call Tori.

Her dream had finally come true. God had answered her prayer and given her a horse of her own, at last.

When a rockin' concert comes to an end,
the audience might cheer for an encore.
When a tasty meal comes to an end,
it's always nice to savor a bit of dessert.
When a great story comes to an end,
we think you may want to linger.
And so we offer …

… just a little something more after
you have finished a David C Cook novel.
We invite you to stay awhile in the story.
Thanks for reading!

Secrets for Your Diary

Secret #1

It was hard for Kate to move to a new town and attend a new school.

Have you ever felt "different" from most of the other kids at school, or been nervous about attending a new school? What did you do to get through that time? Were you able to talk to your parents, a friend, or someone else you trusted about how you felt? If so, what advice did they give you that helped?

Note from Kate

God can help you through any and all hard times, if you're willing to trust Him. He's always ready to listen, so tell Him how you feel. If people in your life are being unkind to you, talk to an adult you trust and ask for help.

Secret #2

Kate was afraid that her friend Tori didn't want to work at the barn. At times that fear made her act or think in ways that she later regretted.

Have you ever misjudged a friend or jumped to conclusions about what a friend might do before you gave him or her a chance to explain? And when have you worried about something before it happened? Write about what eventually happened. If those same situations happened again now, what could you do differently?

Note from Kate

Sometimes we don't think about talking to the person we're upset with and telling him or her how we feel before we get angry. Next time that happens, why not pray first? It will help you stay calm when you talk to your friend. Then ask your friend what he or she meant. It's likely you may have misunderstood his or her actions. Talking about what happened can get you both smiling again.

Secret #3

What Kate wanted more than anything was to have a horse of her own. She thought it would have to come through her parents buying it or her getting a job to pay for it. Instead, the way she got Capri was an unexpected gift.

What would be a dream come true for you? How might you start researching that dream and preparing for it? What steps might you take along the way to keep your dream alive in the meantime?

Note from Kate

Dreams are a wonderful thing, but sometimes they don't come true ... or at least not all at once. I went through a lot of ups and downs before I got a horse of my own. And it didn't come in the way I expected or in the timing I wanted. God knows the desires of our hearts, and He knows about your dreams too. Putting Him first is the right thing to do (Matthew 6:33), because He always has in mind what's best for you.

A Fun Cake for Horse Lovers

Kate's mom baked a horse-head cake for her birthday. You can do the same thing. Be creative. Color your horse the way you want to. And most of all, have fun! I'd never made a horse-head cake before, and mine turned out just fine. If I can do it, so can you!

What you'll need:

 *1 package cake mix (any flavor you like)

 *Vegetable oil (liquid, as noted on cake package)

 *Eggs (as noted on cake package)

 *Water (as noted on cake package)

 *Ready-made chocolate, white, or cream frosting (in tubs, color to your liking)

 *12" x 12" (or 9.5" x 9.5") cake pan

Extras, as desired:

 *1 Hershey's chocolate bar (to cut for ear)

 *Toothpicks

 *1 Oreo cookie or one square dark chocolate (to shape for eye)

 *Black licorice (for mane, eyelashes, halter)

1. Spray cake pan with nonstick spray or grease the pan with oil and then lightly dust with flour, so the cake will come out more easily, without crumbling or breaking.

2. Prepare cake mix according to directions on box. Pour into greased/floured cake pan.

3. Follow directions on cake box for baking and properly cooling the cake.

4. When cake is completely cool, place it on a cookie sheet or large cutting board.

5. Once cake is on cutting board, use the tip of a sharp knife to lightly draw the outline of the horse head in the top of the cake, making sure you don't cut deep. Once you're pleased with the basic shape, proceed to next step.

6. Trim cake into a very basic horse head shape, using square cuts if you're unsure. After shaping the neck and face into basic blocks, go back and round the corners. Your horse head doesn't have to be perfect or shaped like anyone else's. All horses are different, and yours will be unique and wonderful!

7. Once you have your horse head cut out, remove any extra pieces of cake (you can nibble on those as you work!). Frost with your choice of frosting—white or chocolate, or if you want a light brown, mix white and chocolate together. You can also make the horse a pinto by frosting patches of white and patches of brown. Frost the sides first, and

spread the frosting on thick. Place dollops of icing on the top edge and smooth down over the cut sides, connecting the frosting. It's hard not to get crumbs in your frosting, but don't let it worry you if you do. Clean your knife by scraping it on the edge of a bowl occasionally to clear off the crumbs.

8. After your horse head is frosted, it's time to decorate it.

*For the ear, use a piece of chocolate bar, cut into a triangle shape. I had to place several stout toothpicks into the cake behind the ear to hold the ear on. Then I covered the toothpicks with chocolate.

*For the eye: You can use part of an Oreo cookie or a piece of dark chocolate.

*For the eyelashes, mane, forelock, and halter: You can slice tiny pieces of licorice into eyelashes and use full pieces of black licorice for the mane. I didn't have any black licorice on hand, so I chose to darken the chocolate using a melted piece of semisweet chocolate added to my already-chocolate frosting. I dribbled it along the top edge of the neck and the forehead, creating a wispy mane and a forelock. I simply used more frosting and made it stand up higher than the rest. The nostril can be created by making an indentation with the tip of a spoon. You can also use pieces of black licorice to create a halter, if you'd like.

Author's Note

I've been an avid horse lover all of my life. I can't remember a time when I wasn't fascinated with the idea of owning a horse, although it didn't happen until after I married. My family lived in a small town on a couple of acres that were mostly steep hillside, so other than our lawn and garden area, there was no room for a horse. I lived out my dreams by reading every book I could find that had anything to do with horses.

My first horse was a two-year-old Arabian gelding named Nicky, who taught me so much and caused me to fall deeply in love with the Arabian breed. Over the years we've owned a stallion, a number of mares, a handful of foals, and a couple of geldings. It didn't take too many years to discover I couldn't make money in breeding. After losing a mare and baby due to a reaction to penicillin, and having another mare reject her baby at birth, we decided it was time to leave that part of the horse industry and simply enjoy owning a riding horse or two.

Our daughter, Marnee, brought loving horses to a whole new level. She was begging to ride when she was two to three years old and was riding her own pony alone at age five. Within a few years, she requested lessons, as she wanted to switch from

Western trail riding to showing English, both in flat work and hunt-seat, and later, in basic dressage. I learned so much listening to her instructor and watching that I decided to take lessons myself.

We spent a couple of years in the show world, but Marnee soon discovered she wanted to learn for the sake of improving her own skills more than competing, and she became a first-rate horsewoman.

We still ride together, as she and her husband, Brian, own property next to ours. My old Arabian mare, Khaila, was my faithful trail horse for over seventeen years and lived with Marnee's horses on their property, so she wouldn't be lonely. At the age of twenty-six, she began having serious age-related problems and went on to horse heaven in late July of 2013. Now I ride Brian's Arabian mare, Sagar, when Marnee and I trail-ride. I am so blessed to have a daughter who shares the same love as me and to have had so many wonderful years exploring the countryside with my faithful horse Khaila.

If you don't own your own horse yet, don't give up. It might not happen while you still live at home, and you might have to live out your dreams in books, or even by taking a lesson at a local barn, but that's okay. God knows your desire and will help fulfill it in His perfect way.

Acknowledgments

This book has been a brand-new adventure for me—one I never expected, but one I'm so blessed to have experienced. A few years ago I attended a conference in Portland, Oregon, and met Alice Crider, who worked as an editor at a major publishing house. I sat at her table at breakfast, arriving before anyone else, and we started to chat. She asked what I wrote, and I told her my newest book, a historical romance, had released earlier that year. When she heard the title, *Love Finds You in Last Chance, California*, she said she'd spotted it in the conference bookstore and planned to buy a copy, as the picture of the woman on horseback on the cover intrigued her. As we chatted, I discovered we shared a love of horses and riding, and I felt as though I'd found a new friend.

Sometime after the conference, I received an email from Alice saying she'd read my book on the flight home and loved it. She suggested I consider writing a series of horse novels for girls, as so many girls in grade school and middle school have always dreamed of owning a horse. I thanked her and said I'd think about the idea but tucked it back on a mental shelf with no expectation of ever following through. I had already made a change from writing women's contemporary fiction to historical romance and wasn't sure my career would be improved by adding another genre.

Several months later, during a Wednesday-night service at church, our pastor challenged us to pray about the direction our lives were headed and to ask God if there was anything He wanted us to change. I did, and I was surprised at the answer. I felt strongly that He was directing me to write the girls' horse novels, as Alice had suggested.

I was excited and nervous, as I'd never written anything for kids and wasn't sure I could pull it off. I started to write a story (which ended up becoming the second book in this series) and decided to test it on a couple of girls—Kaitlyn Baker, a (then) eight-year-old who attended our church, and eleven-year-old Jessi Hood, my "adopted" (by love) granddaughter, who lived in Alaska. Both girls were given some chapters and asked to give me feedback. They came back with an enthusiastic report, and Kaitlyn, especially, begged for more. Every week she'd meet me at church, asking if I had more chapters and when my book would be published. That little girl's faith and enthusiasm encouraged me and pushed me forward. I planned on naming one of my characters Kaitlyn, until my baby granddaughter was born in April of 2013, and my son and his wife named her Kate. I'm honoring her and Kaitlyn, but using Kate's name instead.

So many others have helped make this series possible: my friends at church, who were excited when I shared God's prompting and offered to pray that the project would find a home, as well as my family, my agent, and my critique group, who believed in me, listened, read my work, and cheered me on. A special thanks goes to Sue Hentges who helped me have a better understanding of autism. There have also been a number of authors who helped me brainstorm ideas for the series or specific sections of one book or the other when I struggled—Kimberly, Vickie, Margaret, Cheryl, Lissa, Nancy—you've all been such a blessing!

But there's a special group of kids I especially want to thank. Two different times I posted on Facebook asking my readers if they had a child who might be willing to read several chapters and give me honest feedback. A number of people responded, and I had my test group of kids. I want to thank Elly, Bella, Payzlie, Cadence, Alexis, Kyra, Hannah, Kasie, Kylie, Crystal, Amber, Haley, Annika, Katelyn, Karli, Jessi, Hailee, Camille, Kayla, and Elena.

I also want to thank the team at David C Cook. I was so thrilled when Don Pape asked if I'd consider sending this series to him to review when I mentioned I was writing it. The horse lovers on the committee snatched it up and galloped with it, and I was so excited! I love working with this company and pray we'll have many more years and books together. Thank you to all who made this a possibility and, we pray, a resounding success! Don, a man who truly believes in my work; Ingrid, the lead acquisitions editor, who kindly allows me to bounce ideas and problems off her; Ramona, my amazing editor, who has a wonderful daughter, Kayla, who also loves horses and offered comments on book two; the amazing marketing team and salespeople, who make sure my books get into your hands; Amy and her awesome graphics team, who do a stellar job on my covers; Jennifer, my copyeditor; Michelle, the wonderful woman who sends out the checks and has become a friend; and everyone else who works behind the scenes that I've yet to interact with—you guys and gals are the best!

If you haven't yet joined my Facebook horse lovers' group for kids, I hope you'll pop over and take a look. You can find a great group at facebook.com. You can also learn more about me and all of my books at www.miraleeferrell.com. Thank you for taking the time to read my new series, and watch for another book in four months!

About the Author

Miralee Ferrell, the author of the Horses and Friends series plus nine other novels, has always been an avid reader. She started collecting first-edition Zane Grey Westerns as a young teen. But she never felt the desire to write books … until after she turned fifty. Inspired by Zane Grey and old Western movies, she decided to write stories set in the Old West in the 1880s.

After she wrote her first novel, *Love Finds You in Last Chance, California*, she was hooked. Her *Love Finds You in Sundance, Wyoming* won the Will Rogers Medallion Award for Western fiction, and Universal Studios requested a copy of her debut novel, *The Other Daughter*, for a potential family movie.

Miralee has many intriguing hobbies. She and her husband, Allen, have built two of their homes and remodeled a one-hundred-year-old craftsman-style house using wood from their own sawmill. Miralee has driven a forklift; stoked the huge, 120-year-old boiler; unloaded lumber; run a small planer; and staked boards in the dry kiln. She loves horseback riding on the wooded trails near her home with her married daughter, who lives nearby, and spending time with her granddaughter, Kate.

Besides her horse friends, she's owned cats, dogs (a six-pound long-haired Chihuahua named Lacey was often curled up on her lap as she wrote this book), rabbits, and even two cougars, Spunky and Sierra, rescued from breeders who couldn't care for them properly.

Miralee and Allen have lived in Alaska, the San Juan Islands, and the Pacific Northwest, where they currently reside. When she isn't writing, riding horses, building/remodeling houses, or hanging out with family, she speaks at women's groups, writing groups, historical societies, and churches about her writing journey.

Miralee would love to hear from you:

www.miraleeferrell.com (blog and website)
www.twitter.com/miraleeferrell
www.facebook.com/miraleeferrell

Sneak Peek at Book Two: Silver Spurs

Chapter One

Odell, Oregon–Upper Hood River Valley
May, Present Day

Kate Ferris hauled back on the reins and brought her Thoroughbred mare to a stop. Her arms ached with the effort. Capri was a lot of horse to keep under control.

The mare tossed her head, and froth flew from her mouth.

Kate patted the mare's neck, her palms sweaty against the dark-red coat. "Easy, girl. Settle down. It's okay." *It's really not okay.* Kate frowned, hoping her voice didn't show her frustration. Determination pushed her forward. No way could she quit and let Capri win this battle. Kate hadn't learned as much as she'd liked in the few lessons she'd taken while working at the English barn a couple of miles from home, but she knew she shouldn't reward Capri by dismounting when the mare wasn't responding to her cues.

The chestnut horse threw her head again and pranced in place.

Kate gave an exasperated sigh. "All right, let's try it again. Slower this time." She nudged her mount into a trot along the rail of the outdoor arena, trying to focus on rising and falling to the beat of the Thoroughbred's long stride. Getting the hang of posting hadn't been easy, but Kate finally had it mastered. At least she hoped she'd mastered it.

Capri pricked her ears, broke into a canter, and ducked her head, throwing Kate off balance. Kate scrambled to stay in her seat, clutching Capri's mane for a moment before gripping the mare's sides hard with her knees. She planted her feet more firmly in the stirrup irons and pulled her horse to a standstill. "I give up." Her shoulders hunched in defeat.

She had been so excited when God brought Capri into her life. Her dream of owning a horse had finally come true! Kate believed it wouldn't be long before she could compete in shows around their area—maybe even qualify for the regional championships in the fall. She'd never expected to own a mare who'd had professional hunter-jumper training.

Problem was, Capri had stood in a pasture for a couple of years when her owner got sick, with no one to keep up what she'd learned. During the past several weeks, Kate's hopes had crashed as she came face-to-face with her own poor horsemanship.

Capri was well trained and smart—maybe too smart. She took advantage of the tiniest bit of hesitation on Kate's part, making it obvious the horse had a mind of her own. She was smart enough to figure out she had a novice in the saddle.

Running the palm of her hand along the sweaty neck, Kate loosened her grip on the reins and urged Capri toward the gate. She leaned over and pushed it open, then rode toward the barn where her mother was working. "Mom! I need you."

Nan Ferris hurried from the open doorway, dusting bits of hay off her jeans. "What is it? I'm trying to organize the tack room."

"I can't do this anymore." Kate lifted her chin, her frustration at Capri bubbling to the surface. She bit her lip to keep it from trembling.

"Do what?" Her mother's hazel eyes narrowed as she stared at the sweating mare. "Have you been running that horse?"

"No. I've been working her in the arena, but I don't know enough, Mom. I'll never get her ready for a show at this rate."

Her mother sighed. "We've discussed this, Kate. You're taking lessons once a week in exchange for cleaning stalls. Your father and I can't afford more right now. Honey … why can't you be thankful you have a horse to love and ride, and not worry about showing?"

Kate swallowed the irritation pressing to escape. Mom didn't understand how important it was to her to learn to ride better.

Sure, she knew the basics, but she'd dreamed of competing ever since her aunt took her to a horse show a couple of years ago. It wasn't like Kate spent a lot of money on clothes. All she'd ever wanted was a horse, but now that she had one, she longed to learn more.

"I've barely started riding a full-size horse instead of Lulu. I love it, but I only have an hour lesson a week. It's not enough, and they aren't teaching me to jump."

Kate heard the complaining in her voice and winced. She knew her dad was working hard to pay for their recent move and to make up for being without a job for so long. With her little brother Peter's autism, and his need for after-school care, her mother had her hands full.

When her mom didn't say anything, Kate swung off her horse and pulled the reins over her mare's head. "I'll walk Capri for a bit and cool her down, then I'll help with the barn." She kicked a dirt clod. "Mom?"

"Yes?"

Kate placed her palm against Capri's neck and grinned. She had the perfect plan … if only Mom would agree. "We have a lot of empty stalls. Can't we advertise and take in boarders? I could clean stalls and feed the horses. And earn money for lessons."

Her mother paused at the big rollaway doors. "Your dad and I considered tearing down this indoor arena or converting it into a storage building. Your grandfather used to board horses here when I was growing up, but his accident is one of the reasons I quit riding. Mother was terrified I'd get hurt too."

"I know, Mom. I've heard that story a million times." Kate bit the inside of her cheek and closed her eyes. Why couldn't Mom understand how important this was? It wasn't like they had miles of trails close by where she could ride. It was boring walking or trotting Capri around in the arena without knowing how to use Capri's training.

She worked to calm her voice. "I'm sorry. It's just that I want this so bad. Would you at least talk to Dad about it? Please?" Her heart raced. "We could have our own business. Maybe even get a professional trainer to give lessons, and we could host shows."

Her mother narrowed her eyes. "Not so fast, young lady. There's a lot to think about. We'd have to check with our insurance agent and see what coverage would cost. The arena needs work, and it means putting out money for hay, shavings, and additional feed. I'll admit it has potential, but it has to work financially. I'll talk to your father when he gets home, if he's not too tired."

"It'll work. I know it will." Kate tugged at her mare's reins. "Come on, Capri. I'm going to make this place shine … after I clean your stall, that is." She shot her mother a look. Mom did a lot around the place, as well as working part-time and caring for Pete. Somehow Kate had to prove she could pull her own weight. "And feed the rabbits and take Rufus for a walk."

A loud bark behind her made Kate jump. She swung around in time to see her ninety-pound German shepherd launch himself across the grass toward her. Capri danced at the end of her reins as the large dog drew closer. Kate held up her hand. "Rufus! Sit, boy!"

Rufus stopped a few inches from Kate's toes. His tongue hung out, and he turned adoring eyes up to meet hers. Then he plopped down and extended a paw.

Kate giggled and dug into her pocket, withdrawing a treat and dropping it into his eager mouth. "Good boy. Did you see that, Mom? I've been working with him, and he finally got it."

Her mother's eyebrows disappeared under her bangs. "Amazing. He's never done that before."

"He's smart." Kate ruffled the fur on his head and scratched behind his ears. "Aren't you, buddy?"

Rufus woofed a reply. Kate could have sworn he was grinning.

"Come on, Rufus. Let's put Capri in her stall." Kate hesitated. "So ... when will you call the insurance agent? Like right now, maybe?"

A tiny smile tugged at the corners of her mom's mouth. "We'll see what your dad has to say first."

"Can I call Tori? She'll be so excited." The reminder of her best friend sent Kate's spirits soaring. Tori loved hanging out at their barn.

"You can talk to Tori, but I'm not making any promises. Even if Dad agrees, there's a lot of work to do before this can happen." She hugged Kate. "I know you're excited, honey, but please don't get your hopes up." Her mother's smile faded.

"Why? What's wrong?"

Her mother sucked in a sharp breath and blew it out slowly. "I'm not sure how your brother will fit into this. It's not like Pete can do anything with horses."

"Aw, Mom!" Kate clenched her fists. Why did Pete always have to come first? Couldn't anything be for her? This had to work. Tori would be in heaven if Kate's family had a riding stable. Tori didn't have a horse, and her family couldn't afford to buy one.

We could ride horses together, and take lessons, and … Kate's thoughts whirled.

Then reality hit. She gritted her teeth. Or not! "That's not fair, Mom! Pete can sit out here and watch while we work. He doesn't have to stay in the house. We shouldn't baby him just because he has autism."

"I'm not trying to, Kate, but I spend a lot of time away from him while I'm at work." Mom smiled. "You pray about it, and so will I. Besides, we don't even know if anyone would want to board their horses here."

Kate tried to force herself to relax. She wrapped Capri's reins around a fence rail, then turned to face her mother. "Sure they will. Tons of people around here own horses. Besides, I've heard about riding programs for special-needs kids. Maybe we could find an instructor who would work with Pete. That could bring in even more business, as well as being good for him." Hope surged through her. "We're in some of the best horse country in the Columbia River Gorge, if not the entire Northwest. There are only two show barns in all of the Upper Hood River Valley, and none in The Dalles or White Salmon."

"Sounds like you've been thinking about this for a while." Her mother tucked a curly wisp of hair behind Kate's ear. "I'll find out what the other barns charge and ask if they're full. Go take care of your horse. Pete's taking a nap, but I'd better check on him."

Kate gazed after her mother as she walked along the path to their two-story house set back in the trees. She loved her six-year-old brother with all her heart, but she hoped he wouldn't be the cause of them not getting to run a boarding stable.

She slapped the riding crop against her leg. Somehow she'd find a way to make this work. Mom spent so much time caring for Pete that Kate often felt left out. Couldn't it be her turn to have something she wanted for a change?

The suggestion to pray about the new project flitted through Kate's mind, but she pushed it away. She loved God, but sometimes He didn't seem very practical. After all, He hadn't kept Pete from being disabled, and He hadn't answered her prayers for more money to help her parents pay the bills. Why should she think He'd care about her dream of owning a show barn and taking lessons?

An instant later, shame washed over her as she was reminded of the miracle of Capri's arrival. God had done that, no mistake. "All right," she whispered heavenward. "Maybe You could help on this request too, if it's not too much to ask?"

Books by Miralee Ferrell

Horses and Friends Series
A Horse for Kate

Love Blossoms in Oregon Series
Blowing on Dandelions Series
Forget Me Not
Wishing on Buttercups
Dreaming on Daisies

The 12 Brides of Christmas Series
The Nativity Bride

Love Finds You Series
Love Finds You in Bridal Veil, Oregon
Love Finds You in Sundance, Wyoming
Love Finds You in Last Chance, California
Love Finds You in Tombstone, Arizona
(sequel to *Love Finds You in Last Chance, California*)
The Other Daughter
Finding Jeena
(sequel to *The Other Daughter*)

Other Contributions/Compilations
A Cup of Comfort for Cat Lovers
Fighting Fear: Winning the War at Home
Faith & Finances: In God We Trust
Faith & Family: A Christian Living Daily
Devotional for Parents and Their Kids

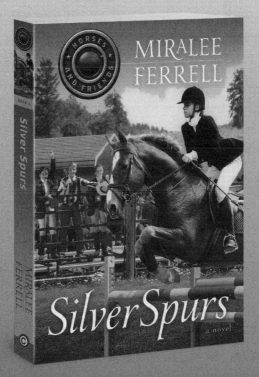

Don't Miss *Silver Spurs,*

Book Two in the Horses and Friends Series

Kate's dream of boarding horses in her family's empty barn and
running her own riding stable starts to feel like a nightmare when her
first customer is Melissa, a mean girl from her school. Kate must
overcome her fears as she looks to God to redeem her dream.